Pioneers of Burra

The Bryar Family Saga

C J Bessell

ISBN: 978-0-6451051-2-4

The characters and events portrayed
in this book are fictitious. Any similarity to
real persons, living or dead, is coincidental
and not intended by the author.

Dedicated to my amazing ancestors

C J Bessell

Prologue

The Pioneers of Burra is the first book in the Copper Road series. It's based on the true story of the Bryar family. They were a family of copper miners who migrated from Cornwall to South Australia in 1857. The purpose of this book is to tell their life story as it unfolded. I've filled in the gaps and missing pieces from their story with historical facts from other sources.

For instance, while it's true that they migrated on board the ships Monsoon and Sumner, there's no record of what life was like on board those vessels. To tell this part of their story I've sourced information from similar voyages. Primarily, this has come from two diaries which were kept by young women who made the journey around the same time. The bulk of information on how the immigration system operated, however, has come from the Emigration Commission's book of regulations.

Similarly, the journey from Adelaide to Burra on the mail coach has come from someone else's experience. So while the coach may not have broken down while Tom and Jenni were on board, it happened to someone else. Wherever possible I've filled in missing information with factual historical events. Likewise, I've used the actual names of other people. Captain Weymess was the captain of the Monsoon and Captain Roach was the captain of the Burra Mine.

I've kept the names and dates of events such as births, deaths and marriages as accurate as possible. I did change one of the main character's names. Jenni Burgess Bryar's name was actually Elizabeth. With so many women in the family named Elizabeth, I changed her name to Jenifred to avoid confusion. The name Jenifred wasn't a randomly chosen name. It was actually Elizabeth's grandmother's name.

When Richard Bryar and his family arrived in Burra I have no idea where they lived, only that it was in the village of Kooringa. At that time, however, miners and their families were living in the dugouts along the creek, and so I thought they might have done so as well. I'm also not sure what Alice and Maryann did for a living. On the passenger list, they were listed as being domestic servants, and so it made sense to me that they would have continued in this line of work in Australia.

There's also no evidence that Richard Bryar bid on his own pitch at the

Burra Mine. However, the records are incomplete, so it's possible. By having Richard bid on his own pitch I've been able to include a lot more information on how the Cornish tribute system worked. It was quite peculiar.

Of course, I've had to make educated guesses about a lot of things as well. Like how they looked and what kind of people they were. So it's mostly how I imagine they might have been. I have tried to base this on how they reacted and behaved to certain events, as well as how events in their lives may have shaped them. So it's not all guesswork.

.∼.

C J Bessell

Chapter 1

Helston Cornwall, July 1856

Tom and his father Richard both jumped off the back of the wagon. After several hours perched on the back of Geordie's dray Tom's legs and back were stiff and cramped. He stretched before heading round to the front of the wagon.

"Thanks for the lift Geordie," said Tom slapping him on the leg. "Will ye be passing back this way later today? If so can ye give us a ride back to Breage?"

Geordie was a scrawny lad of about sixteen years of age who drove the dray for his father's carting business. He was on his way to Falmouth with a load of flour, which was another twelve miles or so on. "I don't know Tom. If I can get this lot unloaded an' pick up somethin' for the return then I might be back this ways later." He took off his battered straw hat and scratched his head. "Anyways ye can surely walk to Breage?"

Tom smiled to himself. Geordie was a good lad. "Aye of course we can. Thanks again Geordie. Give our regards to your Da when you see him."

Tom and Richard were a little early for their meeting with the Emigration Commissions agent. They were not the only ones interested in the offer of free passage to the colonies. The Blue Anchor Inn was bursting at the seams with men. They managed to squeeze inside and found a seat at a small table in the far corner. They ordered a couple of pints before looking around to see if Mr Latimer had yet arrived.

A large table had been set up beside the bar which held several piles of paper, quills and ink. Another similarly arranged was set to the side of the stairs. Sitting behind the larger desk was a balding bespectacled man in his early fifties. That must be Mr Latimer thought Tom. A younger clerk was busy at the other table, already filling in large forms by the looks of it.

Tom indicated to the desk in question. "That looks like Mr Latimer over there Da. Should we introduce ourselves?"

That was not going to be easy. There was already a queue of men, jostling in their obvious eagerness to speak with Mr Latimer. Richard surveyed the scene and then leaned in close to his son to be heard above the noisy crowd.

"We'll be waiting a bit methinks. Drink your ale and relax Tom. We'll be speaking with the man afore the day is out. Not to worry."

Tom tried to relax, but so much nervous energy was pulsing through him, he couldn't sit still. His right leg was jumping up and down in nervous anticipation. Try as he might he couldn't stop the anxious feeling flooding through him. What if they missed out? Tom couldn't afford to miss out.

Things had gone from bad to worse in the last few months for Tom and Jenni. First of all the Wheal Drea mine had simply closed down - said it wasn't worth it anymore and put Tom out of work. He'd managed to pick up some tut work by the luck of knowing the Mine Captain at Carnyorth. The pay wasn't much, and they'd had to let the house go and move back in with his mother and father. The house wasn't big, and adding another two adults and their two young daughters had made things very cramped. They all slept in one room with the girls sharing a trundle under the small window.

He glanced sideways at his father, who appeared to be as calm and relaxed as he could be. "I can't just sit here Da. I'm joining the queue."

In reality, the queue was moving very quickly. Mr Latimer was simply taking down names and asking a couple of questions of each man. There was an older man ahead of Tom with his head bowed low and shoulders slumped. He heard Mr Latimer speaking to him.

"I'm very sorry Mr James, but in order for me to put you on the list for consideration you must have some skill or trade." He paused and looked up at the man, "by your own admission you have none. I'm sorry. Next."

Tom thought Mr James was going to give some sort of argument, but he didn't. He turned and shuffled away.

"Name, age and calling?" asked Mr Latimer without looking up from his paper.

Tom stepped forward. "Thomas Bryar sir. I be five and twenty and a copper miner."

"Excellent," said Mr Latimer, finally raising his eyes to look Tom over. "And will you be having a wife and children Mr Bryar?"

"Aye indeed. I've a wife and two daughters, and another on the way."

Mr Latimer smiled at him showing a row of badly stained teeth in the process. "Just take a seat, Mr Bryar. We'll call for you as soon as we can manage. We'll take down all your details then. Next." He had already dismissed Tom and had his quill poised for the next candidate.

"Um. Can I also give you details for my faather, Richard Bryar?' asked Tom tentatively.

"Of course. Name, age and calling?"

Tom gave the information required to register his father's interest as well, before making his way back to their table. Richard raised a quizzical brow at his son making it clear he hadn't expected him back so soon. "How'd it go? Did you speak to the man?"

"Oh Aye. We've to wait now until he calls for us," replied Tom reaching for his ale. "I expect that will be a while."

It was nearly midday before Mr Latimer began calling names, and early afternoon before Tom heard his name called. He made his way up to the desk and sat down opposite Mr Latimer.

"Now Mr Bryar, you say you're a miner with a wife and two weans," said Mr

Latimer reading off the details he'd taken down earlier. "You're just the sort of candidate the Government's looking for." He glanced up at Tom before continuing. "If you're willing to make certain guarantees, then we can grant you and your family free passage to South Australia."

"What sort of guarantees would they be?"

Mr Latimer now looked him square in the eye. "You would need to sign an undertaking that you and your entire family would remain in South Australia for a space of two years from your arrival."

"I got no problem with that," replied Tom.

"Excellent," said Mr Latimer smiling. "If you do fail in that undertaking you will be required to repay your fares."

Tom nodded in agreement. It seemed like an easy agreement to make. After all, there was very little reason for him to think he'd be wanting to leave South Australia once he got there. According to all reports, there was plenty of work for everyone at the mines in Burra Burra. Several letters had come to the village from Philip Downing who'd immigrated to South Australia the previous year. He wrote in glowing terms of the rich seams of ore within easy reach. Why a man could mine as much as he wanted in no time at all.

"You will be required to make your own way to the port of departure, and at your own expense. Once there, however, the department of Emigration will take care of everything." Mr Latimer handed several pages to Tom. "Now, as to baggage and such for you and your family, it's all written down here what you can take and what you can't. No wines or spirits are allowed and no firearms either Mr Bryar."

Tom took the documents and nodded.

"Now, my clerk Mr Baker will take down the names of your family and their ages so that an embarkation order can be issued. You'll then receive notification in the mail with all your departure details. Make sure you arrive at the port of departure two days before sailing so that you and your family can be inspected by a medical officer."

Mr Latimer shuffled through several more pages before handing another sheet to Tom. "This is a list of clothing and such that you should make sure you have. The more clothing you can take the more comfortable you'll be."

Tom took the list and nodded again as he quickly scanned it. It was quite a long list. It included the need for two pairs of new shoes or boots for himself and Jenni, as well as two pounds of marine soap. He hoped he'd have enough money to buy the number of shirts and stockings that were also required. He was having trouble keeping up with all that Mr Latimer was telling him.

As though he'd read his mind Mr Latimer said. "Not to worry Mr Bryar, the embarkation order will have every detail in it that you need to know." He reached out his hand to shake Tom's. "I wish you the best of luck Mr Bryar. My clerk will take care of the paperwork if you would like to step over to his desk."

Tom stood up feeling rather dazed and shook Mr Latimer's hand. "I thank ye, Mr Latimer."

As he stepped aside and headed for Mr Baker's desk he heard Mr Latimer call his father's name. He hoped to God he'd be successful in obtaining free passage as well. He didn't want to contemplate leaving Cornwall and his family behind forever. It made him think that perhaps he hadn't given Jenni as much sympathy as he should have. After all, she'd be leaving her mother and brother behind, and would likely never see them again. He silently promised himself to do all he could to make up for her loss.

Chapter 2

Jenifred admitted that she loved Tom as much today as she had when she'd married him five years ago. What if she'd had some inkling that he'd want to migrate to the other side of the world though? Would she have been so quick to become his wife? She honestly didn't know, and anyway it was too late.

She smoothed her hands over her swelling belly and held them there. She could only hope the bearn would be born before that day came. The idea of giving birth on board ship was too horrifying to contemplate.

Her mother gave a rather large sniff behind her as she wiped the tears from her face. "Oh, Jenni ye canna possibly go t' the colonies. I've still not got over losing your faather last year. How can ye do this t' me?"

Jenni turned to face her mother. Her tear stricken face and large brown eyes looked imploring at her.

"Please Jenni, don't go," she begged.

Jenifred opened her arms and her mother stepped into her embrace. She hugged her hard against her and allowed her to sob almost uncontrollably in her arms. "I'm so sorry Mamma, but I must go where my husband goes. Must I no? And besides, ye still have Nick and Grace. Ye won't be alone," she soothed. "Ye will be so busy helping Nick with the tavern and the two boys. Oh, Mamma ye will hardly miss us at all."

Elizabeth quieted somewhat. Still hiccupping she stood back from her daughter and looked into her worried grey eyes. "Aye, well there is Nick an' the tavern sure enough," she conceded. "Tis not like having my own daughter though." She knew she couldn't stop her daughter from going with her husband to South Australia, and nor should she. Jenifred was right. Her place was beside Tom, no matter where that was.

"What about Tom's mawther and faather? What do they think of this idea of going off t' the colonies then? I bet they're no more happy about this than me," said Elizabeth crossing her arms and pouting at her daughter.

Jenni had been dreading this question and took a deep breath. "Sit down Mamma I'll make us some tea."

It was Tom's father who'd first shown them the newspaper article advertising-free passage to South Australia.

"Think of it Tom, we could get to Australia for free," he'd said excitedly. "What do ye think?"

Tom had agreed with his father that it could be a perfect opportunity. He and Tom had both gone off to the meeting in Helston to find out if they'd be eligible. They had completed the application form there and then on the spot. Mr Latimer, the Emigration Officer had assured them they were both eligible. It was now just a matter of waiting to find out when passage would be arranged. According to Mr Latimer, that could be as soon as two or three months.

Jenni poured two cups of hot tea and added a little cream to each one before sitting down at the table with her mother. She took a deep breath and tried to calm her racing heart. "Well Mamma, it's not just Tom and me that's going to South Australia." She paused and took a sip from her cup. "Tom's mawther, faather, his sisters and young Richard are coming as well," she blurted.

Elizabeth looked at her daughter incredulously. "What! Tom's whole family is going?"

Jenni nodded. "Yes, Mamma."

"And ye didn't think to ask if I'd like to go as well? Ye are leaving me behind without another thought?" Elizabeth seemed to be too shocked at the news to continue her crying. Her eyes bore into Jenni's like red hot pokers.

Jenni couldn't bear her mother's accusing stare, nor the hurt she saw there. "I'm sorry Mamma, but ye know that's not true. I'm going where my husband decides and ye knows well enough there's naught to be done about it." She took another large gulp of tea. "And besides, would ye truly leave Nick behind all by himself?"

"No," she replied and slumped in her chair - the fight gone out of her. "Ye are right I wouldna like to leave Nick all alone. But Jenni, ye are my only daughter and I may never see ye again. I canna imagine that." She took a sip of her tea and tried to blink back her tears. "I will miss ye and the bearns like mad."

Jenni rose and walked around behind her mother and wrapped her arms about her shoulders. "Aye, and we're going to miss ye like mad as well. I love ye

Mamma, and I think this is the hardest thing I've ever had to do, but there is naught here for Tom."

She kissed the top of her head and sighed. Breaking the news to her mother had gone better than she'd expected. Of course, she wasn't sure how she would feel when the day came to say goodbye to her forever. She pushed it from her mind just as quickly as it came. She would deal with that when the time came and not before.

Chapter 3

It had been several nervous weeks of watching for the mailman, and still, no letters from the Emigration Office had arrived. The entire Bryar household was unsettled and on edge, and Mary was feeling completely frazzled. She knew how anxious her husband and son were feeling, but more importantly, she needed to know if she should start packing.

She glanced at the wooden trunk which was taking up most of the available space in the small sitting room. Richard had ordered two, one for them and one for Tom and Jenni. Tom had managed to somehow stuff theirs under the stairs, but there simply wasn't anywhere to put the other one.

She sighed and ran her hands through her unruly auburn hair for the umpteenth time today. She was starting to look like she'd been pulled through a hedge backwards. Her hair was a frizzy mess. She jammed her cap back on and headed out the front door again to scan the street. Surely, Joe, the errant mailman would have letters today.

She leaned over the small fence and craned her neck. She was quite small and wiry for a woman nearing fifty, and passersby might have thought she was much younger. On closer inspection the telltale signs of ageing were visible. She still had quite a youthful complexion but her once rich auburn hair was now greying at the sides.

She finally caught sight of the mailman coming down the other side of the street. "Ahoy Joe have ye got any mail for me today?" she called waving frantically.

He looked her way and shook his head. "Nay today missus." He continued on his way into the next house without giving Mary another moment.

She was disappointed. Not knowing when they might be leaving on their voyage was really starting to wear her nerves thin. She trudged back inside and into the kitchen, where her eldest daughter Alice and Jenni were baking biscuits. She was greeted by exclamations of delight from three-year-old Beth who had been helping. She was only tall enough with the help of a stool to see over the table, and she had the telltale signs of biscuit making all over her face.

"Grammer! I made bikkie's for Da and Granfer," she squealed excitedly.

Mary smiled at her. "Aye, so I see. Can I have one to try?"

"Mmm me too," she said looking hopefully at her mother.

"Aye, but they'll need to cool first," replied Jenni as she piled hot biscuits onto the cooling rack.

Young Susan immediately popped out from under the table. She'd been busy licking the wooden spoon. "Me Mamma me Mamma," she chanted.

Jenni scooped her into her arms. "Aye, ye too. But first, ye need changing," she said smelling her daughter suspiciously. "Come and wash up Beth then you and Grammer can have a bikkie."

Beth went off happily skipping after her mother.

"I gather there was no mail today Ma," said Alice taking another tray of biscuits from the oven. "Do ye think we'll ever go?" Alice would prefer to remain in Cornwall. Not that she had any particular reason for staying. It was the thought of months at sea with several hundred people she didn't know cramped into a small space. It made her stomach tie itself in knots.

"Oh Aye. We'll be going if your faather has ought to say about it. But it seems not today." She sighed. 'I just canna stand the not knowing."

It was another week before a letter from the Emigration Office finally arrived addressed to Mr Richard Bryar. Mary placed it on the small table in the sitting room where it would have to wait until Richard came home from work. She picked it up and felt it every time she passed, anxious to know what it might contain.

Mary had been on tenterhooks all day waiting for Richard to come home so that it could finally be opened. The wait was driving her mad. It was after supper before Richard finally reached for the large fat envelope. The entire Bryar family gathered around in anticipation.

Richard opened the envelope and drew out a letter and several pages as well as a small booklet. He laid these aside and read the letter out loud to the family.

Emigration Office
13th September, 1856

Dear Mr Richard Bryar,

Following your application for emigration to the colony of South Australia, I am pleased to inform you that passage has been booked for you and your family on board the migrant ship Monsoon. This ship is scheduled to depart the port of Southampton on the 16th December, 1856. Please ensure that you arrive at the port two days prior to your departure date. The enclosed embarkation orders contain all the relevant details.

A list of the minimum outfit required for each member of your family is also enclosed. The average cost is £5 per adult and about half that for children. If you have any difficulty obtaining marine soap it can be purchased at the depot.

Also enclosed is a copy of the current colonisation circular, which contains invaluable information concerning wages, and the cost of provisions in the colonies.

In closing, please allow me to extend to you the best of luck in your endeavours.

Your servant
Mr Stephen Walcott
Commissioners Agent

"December," said Mary letting out the breath she'd been holding. "I can only hope tis enough time to get everything in order."

She looked around at her family. The anxious look Tom had been sporting for the last few weeks hadn't changed. Alice looked resigned, whereas fifteen-year-old Maryann appeared to be very apprehensive. Twelve-year-old Lizzie appeared to be uninterested. Young Richard on the other hand was beside himself with excitement. She supposed the thought of months at sea on a ship must seem very exciting to a nine-year-old boy. How was she going to stop him from falling overboard in his enthusiasm she didn't know. Mary finally turned her attention to her husband and realised he was looking vacant and staring into space.

"Is everything awright love?"

Richard turned his vacant expression on his wife. "Oh aye," he replied vaguely.

"Well, ye don't seem awright."

He smiled at her. "Tis only that I thought we'd all be going together like." He turned to his son. "Unless your letter arrives in the next day or so Tom, I canna think how we're going to be sailing on the same ship. I just never expected that we wouldna be all going at once."

Mary hadn't realised that of course, Tom would be getting his own letter. They had applied at the same time on the same day, but they'd put in separate applications. She turned to her husband in alarm. "But that canna be! We canna be going off and leaving Tom and Jenni and the girls behind. What if his letter doesna come?"

"Don't worry Ma, it will come," replied Tom. "Even if we travel on a different ship, we'll be going too. South Australia. Mr Latimer assured me that I was eligible."

Mary didn't think he really believed that. He looked more anxious than ever, but she didn't want to add to his worries. "I'm sure ye be right Tom. I agree with your faather though, I just never expected us to be going separate like."

Richard nodded in agreement. "Well there is naught to be done but wait for Tom's letter to arrive." He folded the letter and put it back in the envelope with the

31

Embarkation Orders. He handed the Outfit list to his wife. "Ye and the girls can use this list to make sure we've all got what we need to take in the way of clothes. And ye may have to buy some new ones if we're short. Ye may need to buy a few of the other items as well."

Mary took the list and quickly scanned it. It was a rather long list and included the number of each type of garment that would be required for everyone. It also included a list of household items such as tin plates and cutlery as well as sheets and blankets. Mary had no idea they would have to supply their own eating implements. She also noted the need for a strong chest with a lock.

"Well apart from that trunk that will go in the hold," she said indicating to the wooden trunk taking up half the sitting room. "We'll also be needing a strong chest or two to put our personal belongings in. You'll have to get them for me, Richard. Then I'll start to pack."

Richard nodded. "Don't ye worry none Mary, I'll get them. Ye best start to go through that list though. But not tonight. Tis time for my bed and yours as well," he said looking around at his children. "Say your goodnights and don't forget your prayers."

Later when Mary was finally in her bed wrapped in Richard's arms she allowed her fears to surface. "Richard, I'm afeard to leave Tom and Jenni behind. What if they don't follow?" She couldn't possibly leave not knowing when or if her eldest son and his family would join them.

"Don't fear Mary. Tom's letter will arrive in a day or two, and then we'll know when they're to leave as well," he squeezed her tight in his arms. "They'll follow I promise ye."

She allowed his words to soothe her. "Aye, I'm sure ye be right."

They were silent for a while and Mary was surprised when Richard spoke again. She was sure he'd fallen asleep. "Would ye like to go to St Hilary to say goodbye to the bearns afore we leave? I thought we could go Sunday next if ye'd like."

Mary turned to face him. Even in the dim light, she could see that even after all these years he was still haunted, as was she, by the loss of their bearns. They'd lost five of their children and neither of them had understood why God had so forsaken them.

"Oh aye. Ye know very well I wouldna leave without saying a last goodbye to them," she replied. "But just the two of us....together."

Richard hugged her close. "Aye just the two of us."

Chapter 4

November, 1856

Tom sighed as he began climbing the last ladder out of the mine. His thigh muscles were burning from climbing the ladders from the bottom of the pit, but he kept on. Finally, he could see shards of daylight as he heaved himself to the top of the shaft. Regardless of his complaining legs, he was elated. It had been his first full shift back mining ore for tribute money.

After several months of tut work, digging shafts, he'd managed to join a pare of five who'd won their bid for a pitch at the Rose Wheal mine. It was tin mining, but it looked like it would be a profitable enterprise. He was delighted.

After eight hours underground the cold November wind took him by surprise. He shivered, and wrapped his coat tighter about himself and pulled his woollen hat down around his ears as he began the two-mile walk home.

Although he was a lot happier with his employment situation, it had not reduced the overall anxiety he was feeling. He still hadn't received any news from the Emigration Office and was worried he hadn't secured free passage. He kept his thoughts to himself while assuring his mother and wife that everything would be fine. He wasn't sure if they believed him anymore either.

A cold gust of wind suddenly whistled passed and he pulled his hat more firmly down over his ears and trudged on. He'd been living with the knot in his stomach for so long now that he barely noticed it. How he wished he could be calm and relaxed in the face of the unknown like his father. No point wishing, it only made him more apprehensive.

Tom was nearly passed the Red Lion Inn when he decided to call in for a pint. He stepped inside and was immediately enveloped in the warmth from the blazing fire. Taking off his hat and unbuttoning his coat he made his way over to the main bar where he could see his brother-in-law. The Inn wasn't too busy for the time of day. There were a couple of older men in deep conversation at one table, and a group of four over by the fireplace. Nick was serving another at the bar, but

Tom thought he ought to have time to talk over a pint.

Nick looked up as Tom sidled up to the bar. He smiled warmly at him and Tom let out the breath he'd been holding. He hadn't spoken with Nick since deciding to emigrate and hadn't been too sure what his reception would be. He was taking his only sister to the other side of the world and they would likely never see each other again.

Tom smiled back, "Have ye got time for a pint?"

"Oh aye," replied Nick as he poured two pints and placed one on the bar for Tom. "Joe can ye mind bar?" he called to a young dark-haired lad who'd just arrived carrying an armful of logs for the fire.

He looked at Nick and nodded enthusiastically. "Aye Mr Burgess."

"Good...come on out back Tom where we can hear ourselves."

Tom followed his brother-in-law down a narrow passage beside the stairs. At the end of the passage was a dark wooden door which had etched into it in large lettering, Private. Nick opened it and led Tom into the private part of the Inn which he and Grace and his two sons occupied.

Tom barely had time to brace himself before his two young nephews threw themselves at him, accompanied by squeals of delight. "Uncle Tom! Uncle Tom!"

He managed to put his ale down and then wrapped his arms about the two young boys. "Willie and James ye wee rascals. Ye have both grown since I saw ye last. What are ye feeding them?" He ruffled their dark wavy hair, so like their father's. In fact, they were both the spitting image of Nick.

"Run along boys, your Uncle Tom and me would like some peace now," said their father smiling at them.

"But Da...," Willie began to complain and was joined by his younger sibling's imploring look at their father.

"Leave us in peace I say," said Nick frowning at his sons. "Go on with ye."

"I'll see ye afore I go," promised Tom.

Looking somewhat appeased the two boys left their father and Uncle to themselves. "Bye Uncle Tom," young Willie called over his shoulder as they left.

The two men settled themselves comfortably in the small sitting room. Tom waited for Nick to speak first. He knew his brother-in-law would be direct. He wasn't surprised when he asked him if it was true, that they were leaving for the colonies.

"Well I've not yet received the embarkation order," replied Tom. "But aye, we intend to go. Sooner rather than later I expect."

Nick sat thoughtfully for a few moments. "Well I canna say I'm happy about it, but I know Jenni would follow ye to the ends of the earth. I will miss all of ye, and I know Grace feels the same way." He paused and looked directly at Tom. "I've not yet told the boys what ye intends. Tis best to wait until ye knows for sure."

Tom nodded. He knew what pain he was causing Jenni's family, and he was sorry for it. But he had to think of himself and his family first. "Well, I expect we'll be leaving early in the New Year. The rest of my family goes afore Christmas," Tom informed him. "Best tell the boys soon and give them a chance to get used to the idea."

Nick drained his glass. "I'll wait a bit methinks. Unless of course, my mawther decides to tell them first." He groaned. "I canna imagine her ever being happy about you taking Jenni and the bearns to the other side o' the world."

Tom knew that for sure. His mother-in-law had made it quite plain to him that she thought he was a monster for taking

Jenni and the girls away. He hoped Nick could find some way to appease her.

The door opened and Grace entered in a flurry of cloak and skirts. "Joe's doing a proper job out there, but tis getting busy in the bar. He'll be needing a hand," she said without looking at her husband. She removed her bonnet and cloak before turning around. She was surprised to see they had company. "Tom! How nice to see ye, I've just come from your place."

Tom rose from his chair and greeted Grace with a hug and an affectionate kiss on her cheek. "Ye are looking very well... Nick and I were just discussing when we might be leaving for the colonies," said Tom. "But I'll be off now. Thank ye for the ale."

Grace gave her husband a quick kiss in greeting before turning to Tom. "I've been visiting Jenni. The mail you've been expecting from the emigration arrived this morning. Why your Ma and Jenni are in such a spin about it. They can hardly wait for you to get home."

Tom could hardly believe his ears, and couldn't hide the relief that came flooding through him. The knot in his stomach that he'd been living with for weeks evaporated, and he grinned stupidly at her. "Are ye sure? Was it a fat brown envelope?"

"The very same," she replied patiently. "Ye best be getting yeself home quick smart."

"I canna say I'm very happy about the news," grumbled Nick. "Twould appear that ye are going then, ye and Jenni."

Tom smiled grimly at his brother-in-law. "Aye. I'm that sorry about it, for ye and Jenni I mean. But twill be a better life for us all." He bid them both goodbye and stopped to hug his two nephews who were waiting for him on the front step of the Inn.

"Bye Uncle Tom," they both called after him as he made his way down the street towards home.

Tom couldn't wait to get home. His mind was racing and his heart appeared to be beating in time with his footsteps. He told himself he was presuming it was the same letter his father had received. But what if it wasn't? His stomach clenched uncomfortably at the thought.

He was opening the small wire gate and approaching the front door before he knew it, and couldn't recall exactly how he'd got there. He was already removing his hat and coat as he went in the front door. He hung them on the rack and headed towards the sound of feminine voices. His mother and Jenni were in the kitchen preparing supper.

Jenni looked up as he entered and smiled widely at him, her soft grey eyes alight with obvious excitement. "Tom. How was ye first day back at the mine?"

He brushed her aside. "Never mind that. Where is it? Grace tells me the letter arrived at last!"

"Aye, it has," his mother answered as she handed the fat brown envelope to him. "And I'm ever so glad. Open it Tom so we can know what's to do."

He slit open the envelope and putting everything else aside read the top letter. Jenni and Mary both held their breath in anticipation of what news it held.

Tom finally let out a long slow breath. "We're to go aboard the Sumner in February," he announced. Grinning like a shot fox he grabbed Jenni and hugged her tight. "Oh thank God! I didna like to tell ye I was so afeared we'd not be going." Suddenly tears stung his eyes, and he hugged her even closer. "I know this will be bittersweet for ye though Jenni."

She held him and stroked his hair. "Hush. Twill be awright," she crooned. "I go with a glad heart for us and our bearns."

Chapter 5

12th December, 1856

For the last few weeks, the entire household had been a flurry of activity. Mary had gone over the outfitting list at least a hundred times to ensure that she hadn't missed a thing. Clothing and footwear for herself, Richard, Lizzie and young Richard had been packed into two chests. Another was filled with linen, blankets and utensils as well as various personal items. Clothing and linen for Alice and Maryann were in another.

The embarkation order for the two eldest girls made it clear that on board ship they'd be in the single women's quarters. Mary wasn't at all happy about this arrangement and had berated Richard about it for weeks. There was simply nothing he could do to change it. Mary had finally relented and packed their belongings separately.

She was now adding last-minute items to the large trunk which had been taking up most of the available space in the sitting room for months. In it, she'd packed a set of their best clothes and new boots for everyone. Richard's tools were packed in there as well. She was now stuffing in whatever else she could fit in the way of pots and pans and household items. Anything she thought they might need once settled in their new home in Burra Burra.

"I willna be able to close that trunk if ye put anything else in there," complained Richard as he attempted to close it. Although it had a rounded lid which would allow for overfilling, Mary had gone way beyond the limits. "Ye will have to take out those last two baking pans Mary, it willna close otherwise." He pushed down harder on the lid, but it was no use.

After a bit more arguing and Richard's failed attempts to close the trunk, Mary finally conceded that some items would have to remain behind. She removed several baking pans and a large kettle before the lid was able to be closed. Richard tightened the leather straps and attached and secured the lock.

Richard and Tom heaved it outside to the waiting dray. The other four chests had already been loaded and once the trunk was on board there was only enough room for Tom and young Richard to perch on the back. Richard jumped up front with the driver for the short drive to Porthleven. They were meeting the merchant vessel Charlotte which would take them onto Southampton.

"I'll send Tom back with the dray for ye and the girl's, Mary," Richard called to his wife. "Make sure ye be ready and waiting." He smiled and waved to her as they headed off.

Richard didn't normally worry unnecessarily about things. Today though he was feeling very apprehensive as they went down the road. He would be glad when they were all aboard the Charlotte and on their way. I'll be awright then he convinced himself. If there was any delay in getting to Southampton then they might miss their ship to South Australia. That was what was bothering him he concluded. Maybe we should have gone by coach and rail instead he mused...too late now.

Porthleven was only a small fishing village but it had a large safe harbour which catered to the needs of the ships which brought in coal, lime and timber. Many merchant vessels also called into Porthleven to take their exports of fish, china clay and tin.

Richard scanned the quayside for the Charlotte. He had received a message from Captain Harcourt yesterday afternoon advising him that the Charlotte had docked. The Captain had stipulated that he wanted Richard and his family aboard before noon. He spied her easily enough tied to the wharf between a couple of fishing vessels. He pointed her out to Geordie, who clicked the horses into action and they headed towards the waiting ship.

As soon as the dray stopped Richard jumped off the dray and started towards the gangplank. A rather burly seaman stopped him with a hand on his shoulder just as he was about to step aboard. "Hold up there mate. What business do ye have?"

Richard was momentarily startled. He'd been so intent on boarding he hadn't noticed the seaman lounging nearby. "Oh!" he exclaimed. "The name's Richard Bryar. Captain Harcourt is expecting me and my family. We're passengers."

"Everything awright Da?" enquired Tom as he sidled up beside his father and glared at the sailor.

The seaman immediately relaxed. "Welcome aboard Mr Bryar. I'm Second Mate, John Marsden," he said grinning at Richard. "The Captain will be glad ye've arrived afore time."

"Well, I've still got to send the dray for the rest of my family."

"That's alright, there's plenty o' time," he replied. "I'll have yon baggage brought aboard for ye." He called out to several hands to get the luggage from the dray. "Come this way Mr Bryar, I'll show ye to your cabin."

Richard followed Mr Marsden on board with young Richard at his heels. The Charlotte was a two-masted ketch, and young Richard appeared to be weighing up the possibility of climbing the tallest one. His father grabbed him by the shoulder and headed him towards the main hatch.

They followed Mr Marsden down a short ladder which led to a narrow passageway. He opened a small door halfway down and stood back to allow Richard and his son to enter. The cabin was rather small and cramped with two narrow bunks and a small table set under a porthole.

They were likely to be only spending one or two nights on board the ketch, so Richard thought it was most suitable. He presumed there was another cabin for himself and Mary.

"Thank ye, Mr Marsden," said Richard. "Twill suit the bearns just fine methinks."

"Oh aye," he replied. "The cabin for yeself and Mrs Bryar be right opposite." He opened the door on the other side of the passage to reveal an even smaller cabin with accommodation for Richard and Mary.

A young cabin boy appeared in the doorway. "S'cuse me, Mr Marsden. The clay shipment's arrived and ye be needed on deck."

Mr Marsden excused himself and Richard decided to go and wait on deck for Tom to return with Mary and the girls. He was grateful the apprehension he'd been feeling earlier had dissipated. He wasn't at all used to feeling so ill at ease.

It was cold up on deck, and he shivered as he wrapped his arms about himself. It was grey and overcast and he hoped any drizzle would stay off until the rest of the family had arrived. Where was young Richard? He suddenly realised that he wasn't with him. He quickly looked around the deck, no sign of him. Some crew were lowering a load of clay into the hold and he felt sure young Richard would be with them. He only hoped he hadn't fallen into the hold.

He rushed over just in time to see Richard lean over the gaping hole while hanging onto the hatch with one hand. "Richard! Get back!" he yelled.

Young Richard looked up at his father quite nonplussed. He pulled himself upright and stepped away from the hold. "Tis awright Da, I wouldna fall."

Richard grabbed his son by the scruff of his neck and propelled him towards the railing. "Stand over there and keep an eye out for your brother returning," he said scowling at him.

Thankfully they didn't have to wait long. Richard breathed a sigh of relief to see Mary and the girls coming up the gangplank. He could hand responsibility for young Richard over to his wife - and did so gladly.

"Keep a close eye on him, Mary, he almost fell in the hold." He put his arm around her waist to steady her as she stepped onto the deck.

Tom was also coming on board with two-year-old Susan in his arms. Alice had young Beth by the hand and was holding her back from skipping up the gangplank. He was glad Tom had brought his girls down to wave goodbye. Tom and Jenni would have their hands full with Beth on board a ship for several months. He groaned. He didn't know how he was going to keep young Richard out of trouble for the next few months either.

Mary put her arm around her young son's shoulder. "Stay close now, I don't want ye getting into trouble with the Captain. Don't go touching anything ye are not supposed to...Awright?"

Young Richard grudgingly nodded his head and grumbled. Mary hoped he'd at least try not to get into trouble.

It was starting to drizzle light rain when the Second Mate, Mr Marsden, came along and invited them to all take respite in the saloon. The cook had prepared a pot of hot tea for which Mary was most grateful.

"We'll be underway within the hour," he advised them. "Not to worry, I'll let ye know in plenty o' time so as ye can say your goodbyes." He headed straight back out barking orders to the crew as he went.

Richard sighed and looked around at his family. So this was it, they were really leaving. "Now don't forget Tom, old Jonas is taking all the furniture, but not until the end of January. And make sure he pays ye the full amount," said Richard. Old Jonas could certainly be trusted to strike a fair

deal. Richard also knew that he was a
cunning old fox and could try one on Tom
if he was unwary. "He's agreed to take it all
for twenty pounds, and not a penny less."

"Aye Da, don't worry I'll make
sure," replied Tom. "And I know you've
paid the rent until then as well. Don't
worry."

Richard was confident Tom would
take care of it. "Aye I'll leave it to ye," he
said resigned to the fact that there was
nothing else he could do in any case.
"When we get to the Burra Burra I'll try
and send a letter for ye with our address and
such. If I can I'll leave it in care of the
Emigration there."

"Aye, but don't worry Da. The
Burra Burra canna be so big that we willna
find ye, aye."

Richard nodded. Tom was right, it
couldn't be so big that they wouldn't find
them. In any case, Richard expected to be
working at the local mine by the time Tom
and his family arrived. They could always
enquire after him there.

The door opened letting in a draft of
cold damp air. "Time to go, we be hoisting
the sails just as soon as ye've said ye
farewells," said Mr Marsden poking his
head into the saloon.

Richard felt his heart clench as Tom began hugging and kissing his sisters farewell. He knew it would only be a matter of a few months and they'd all be together again, but those months apart could be very hazardous. Many ships made the crossing to Australia, but he knew very well that some never made it. He hoped and prayed they'd all arrive safe and in one piece.

Tom gathered his mother in his arms and hugged her tight. Richard could see the tears in both their eyes, and swallowed hard as he felt his own eyes welling. He wrapped his two granddaughters in his arms and kissed them both soundly. "Come say goodbye to ye Grammer as well." The two little girls obediently grabbed their Grammer and kissed her soundly.

Finally, Tom came to his father. "Goodbye Da and safe travels," he said as he gripped him tightly. They stood hugging for a long moment before Richard pulled away.

"Take care son, and Gods speed to ye as well."

The crew of the Charlotte pulled the gangplank aboard as soon as Tom and the girls were safe on the quay. Richard could see Beth and Susan waving gaily at them, as he too raised his hand in farewell. The

Charlotte lurched as the winds took her sails and Richard felt his stomach lurch with her. He paid no heed, as he continued to feast his eyes upon his ever diminishing son and granddaughters. They were through the sea wall and headed for Devon before he pulled himself away from the railing.

Chapter 6

The journey from Porthleven to Southampton was short and uneventful. The Charlotte made good time, and on the evening of the 13th of December, they docked at the Southampton wharf.

Captain Harcourt suggested they remain on board for the night rather than spending it in the Emigration Depot. Richard was keen to disembark and have solid ground under his feet, but Mary won out and they spent another night on board the ketch.

In the end, Richard was only sorry they couldn't have stayed on the Charlotte. Accommodation in the Emigration Depot consisted of several large dormitories. Each one was capable of housing about twenty families each. It wasn't that the accommodation was inadequate. The dormitory was light and airy and quite cosy, if somewhat cramped. They had very little privacy with the sleeping berths two stories high. Richard and Mary had the bottom bed and Lizzie and young Richard the upper bunks. There was a large mess hall and their meals were prepared for them. The big problem was that the single women were accommodated in a separate dormitory.

Mary sat with her head in her hands sobbing. Richard had his arm wrapped around her shoulders crooning softly. She knew he was there but ignored his comforting words. It was bad enough being separated from Thomas and Jenni, but now her girls as well. It was all too much, and all of a sudden the thought of leaving her homeland for the unknown seemed an insane idea.

"I want to go home," she finally managed to say between gulps of air. "I don't want to do this anymore."

Richard tightened his grip on her. "No. Ye are just afeard is all, twill be awright." He tried to impart a meaningful look to Lizzie and Richard. They were also looking rather glum and downhearted and not taking his hints.

Lizzie finally seemed to take his meaning. "Aye, twill be awright Ma. Ye can go and see Alice and Maryann. I'll come with ye."

"There ye go. That be an excellent idea," said Richard grasping onto the idea in the hopes that it would allay Mary's fears. "You two go off and see that Alice and Maryann are awright and settled. While you're gone, Richard and I'll see if we can get that marine soap we need."

Mary took several more large gulps of air before she managed to stifle her sobs. She had let the situation overwhelm her and she was sorry to have worried Richard and the children so. She could see that her outburst had scared Lizzie and young Richard. She summoned up all her courage to be strong. Her family meant the world to her and she would die for any of them. For now, though, she'd put on a brave face in the hopes of assuring them that all would be well.

"Aye, that be a grand idea," she said smiling weakly at them. "Come on then Lizzie, let's go see if we canna find them."

The single women's dormitory was in an adjoining building separated from the main depot by a large courtyard. The chill hit Mary as soon as she stepped outside and she pulled her cloak more firmly about herself. Taking Lizzie by the hand they made their way across the courtyard and inside. They were met by a rather stern-looking middle-aged woman who was the Matron of the single women's dormitory. She introduced herself as Mrs Berkshaw and her face softened when she smiled at them. Mary realised she was far friendlier than she had first appeared.

Mary explained who she was and who she was wanting to see.

"Oh aye," replied Mrs Berkshaw. "Twould be best if ye follow me and I'll show ye where they are." Without waiting for a reply she headed off down the corridor calling behind her, "come along then."

Mary and Lizzie hurried along the corridor until they caught up with the remarkably quick Mrs Berkshaw.

"Just down here me dearies," she said opening the door to the dormitory. She led them between the bunks until she was near the end of the first row. "There they are. I'll leave ye to your visit then," she said indicating to the two girls. Alice and Maryann were sitting on one of the lower bunks looking somewhat lost.

"Ma! Lizzie!" exclaimed Maryann leaping to her feet. She grabbed her mother in a tight hug and then Lizzie. "We didna know what to do, or where we might find ye."

Mary hugged her daughter in return and then reached for Alice to hug her too. Alice seemed like a limp rag in her arms.

"What's amiss? Are ye awright Alice?" she enquired holding her at arm's length to get a better look at her. "Are ye feeling poorly?" She did seem to be a little pale and Mary quickly felt her forehead. No, there was no sign of fever.

"I'm awright Ma," she replied.

"Well ye certainly seemed awright a few hours ago when we got here, but ye don't seem awright now. Tell me what's amiss then?" Mary prodded her.

Eventually, after more prodding and coaxing Alice admitted what was troubling her. She was such a shy girl, and she was uncomfortable sharing the large dormitory with so many strangers. Her stomach was tied up in knots and she was feeling quite sick at the thought of sleeping there the night. She'd be far happier if she could be with the rest of the family.

Mary's heart went out to her daughter, but there was naught she could do to ease her discomfort. "Oh, Alice at least ye have Maryann with ye for company," she said trying to console her. "How about we go and see if we canna get a cup of tea to help settle ye."

Mrs Berkshaw was sympathetic to Alice's plight and pointed them in the direction of the mess hall. They were able to get a pot of tea from the cook. No sooner had they settled down to a nice soothing cup of tea than two girls arrived and asked to join them. As it turned out Mrs Berkshaw had sent them to introduce themselves. They were sisters, Christian and Julia McDonald. Christian explained that they would also be travelling on board the Monsoon with their parents. They were from Scotland and Mary found their accents enchanting.

In no time at all, they were chatting gaily with Alice, Maryann and Lizzie. Mary heaved a sigh of relief. She would have to remember to thank Mrs Berkshaw for sending the McDonald sisters to their table. What a godsend.

It was nearing supper time by the time Mary and Lizzie made their way back to their dormitory. Mary was feeling much better. She was hopeful that Alice would overcome her anxiety with the help of the McDonald sisters.

Mary was pleased to see Richard visibly relax when he saw her. "So the girls are awright, and I can see that ye are much better yourself Mary," he said as he helped her remove her cloak.

Mary leaned against her husband and breathed a sigh. "The girls will be awright. And I'm so sorry for adding to your worries...I'm fine now."

"Da and I have the soap," chimed in young Richard. "We packed it in with the blankets and such."

"Ah yes," said Richard ruffling his son's hair. "And we've been told to report to Dr Griffin tomorrow morning before breakfast for inspection. I expect we'll be able to board the ship after that."

Mary felt quite exhausted, but she was feeling much more at peace. She smiled to herself. Her family was far more resilient than she imagined they could be. Even with Alice's anxiety and her own fears for the future, she realised that as long as they stood together they would be fine. The next few months onboard a cramped vessel at sea was going to be trying, but a new life awaited them. It would be worth it.

Chapter 7

Southampton, 16th December 1856

It was nearly ten o'clock before Richard, Mary and the children returned to their dormitory. They'd enjoyed an ample breakfast of toast with ham and good coffee. The first thing they noticed on their return was that their luggage had been removed.

Mr and Mrs O'Loughlin, who had the accommodation next to them, were sitting on the lower bed and smiled as they approached. Their two daughters, Kate and Honora peered down from the top bunks.

"Mr O'Loughlin, did ye see what happened to our baggage?" Richard inquired hopefully.

Patrick O'Loughlin rose from the bed and grinned at Richard. He was a small man, only reaching Richard's chin, but he was well built and Richard imagined well muscled. His wife Catherine was even shorter. She was an attractive woman with a mop of black curly hair and bright dancing eyes. Richard thought they were both well into their forties.

"Aw aye. They've taken it all aboard ship like. Mr Slater says as how he'll be back to take us all aboard as well. Twill not be long now methinks," he replied in his lilting Irish accent.

Richard thanked him and settled down to wait. He imagined it was going to be rather chaotic getting nearly four hundred people boarded. He couldn't imagine how they would match them up with their baggage. Of course, they weren't the first lot of migrants to do this and so he concluded that the Emigration Commission must know what they were doing. At least he hoped they did.

Mr Slater returned to their dormitory before noon. "Now if I can have your attention if you please," he said in a booming voice. Most people stopped what they were doing and looked in his direction. "You will be boarding your vessel in the same order that you are in now. Just follow the person ahead of you. This is Mr Wilcox, Second Mate of the Monsoon. Please follow him and he will direct you to your berths. Now if you please, starting with you," he said indicating a young couple at the end of the first row.

Those at the head of the row got to their feet ready to leave. "Please try and keep up," called Mr Wilcox as he headed out of the dormitory.

Richard and Mary were about halfway down the row and had a minute or so to get organised. They readied themselves to follow Mr and Mrs Pritchard who were in front of them. Pushing Lizzie and young Richard ahead of them they started filing out of the depot in an orderly manner. The chilly wind hit them as soon as they stepped outside - its icy fingers sticking into any bare flesh. Richard shivered and pulled his woolly hat further down over his bare ears.

It was only a short walk across the docks and they hurried to keep up. Richard tucked Mary's hand into his elbow as they stepped aboard the Monsoon. It was a three-masted vessel and much larger than anything Richard had been on before. He could feel the slight movement of the deck beneath his feet as the ship rose and fell on the swell. His stomach squirmed in response. He swallowed and took in several large gulps of air before following Lizzie and young Richard below.

It took a moment for his eyes to adjust to the dim interior. Both sides of the ship were lined with two tiers of berths. These were sectioned off into compartments, each accommodating eight people. Down the centre of the aisle were long tables with benches on either side. Richard thought the height between the decks was no more than six feet and he was glad he wasn't any taller. They went almost halfway down the aisle before he saw the Second Mate, Mr Wilcox. He was standing in the middle of the aisle and gestured them to a compartment on the port side of the ship.

Richard stepped into the very cramped space. It was arranged very similarly to the Emigration Depot. Richard and Mary's bed on the bottom and two bunks above for Lizzie and young Richard. There was just so little space. He noticed their chests had been stacked beneath the bulkheads. He smiled to himself. He was really surprised that it was so organised and orderly.

They would not have the compartment to themselves though. There was accommodation for another four people. No sooner had he made this realisation than the O'Loughlin family filed into the compartment as well. He could barely move as he was pressed up against the bunks.

He noticed that Mary wasn't looking at their accommodation in a very favourable light. She had screwed up her nose and looked rather displeased. Richard was feeling nauseous and he just had to get out of the compartment. "I'll just be out there." He didn't wait for Mary to acknowledge him or respond, and pushed roughly past Mr O'Loughlin with a grunt of apology.

He sat down on the bench and took in several large gulps of air. It wasn't helping, and even though the day was cold he was sweating profusely. God, how was he going to survive three or four months of this? He groaned and put his head in his hands. Funnily enough, he felt himself calming down. The sick feeling he had experienced in the compartment was subsiding, thank goodness. He kept his head down for several more minutes and breathed slowly.

"Are ye awright Da?" asked young Richard as he leaned over his shoulder and peered at him.

"I will be. Just give me a bit."

"Oh...well Ma wants the key to the chest so as she can get the beds made up."

Richard reached into his pocket pulled out his keys and handed them to young Richard. "Twill be one of the long brass ones. Be careful ye don't lose them."

"Don't worry, I willna lose them," replied young Richard. He took the keys from his father and went back into the small compartment.

Mr O'Loughlin and his youngest daughter Honora sidled up beside Richard. "Tis jammers in there," he said indicating their shared compartment. "Me an' Honora are going up on deck for some air, Mr Bryar. Would ye care to join us like?"

"Thank ye kindly, but no I best stay here for a bit," he replied looking up at him. "Please call me Richard."

Mr O'Loughlin smiled at him showing a rather large gap between his front teeth. "Aye, and ye must call me Paddy. Well, we shall see ye on our return no doubt. Come along Honora."

After they'd gone Richard got to his feet and went back into the cabin. He was feeling much better. He could still feel the ship heaving gently beneath his feet, but his stomach had decided not to heave with it. He breathed a sigh of relief.

Mary and Lizzie were busy making up their berths, as was Mrs O'Loughlin and her daughter Kate. Mary turned to look at him as he entered. "Ye are looking much brighter Richard. That's good. Hand me another blanket outta the chest will ye. Tis so cold I think we'll be needing more than one tonight."

He obliged her. "Young Richard and I can finish this off, Mary. Do ye think ye should go and check on Alice and Maryann? I'd like to be sure they're safe on board aye."

Mary scowled at him. "We are just about finished thank ye all the same."

He glanced at Mrs O'Loughlin. She appeared to be very intent on smoothing every crease out of a rather flowery counterpane. He moved closer to Mary and put his arm around her shoulders. He hoped the gesture would be received as an 'I'm sorry.' He felt her sag and lean into him and let out the breath he'd been holding.

"I know this isn't going to be easy," he whispered. "But we canna be getting vexed with one another."

She smiled weakly up at him and kissed him on the cheek. "Aye. I'll go and check on the girls, ye finish up here then. Come with me Lizzie we'll see if we canna find your sisters."

There wasn't much more to do. He handed two blankets up to young Richard who was tucking the last sheet into the top bunks. "Spread them out as best ye can."

A young steward popped his head into their compartment. "S'cuse me, sir, ma'am. I'm the Steward in charge of this deck. Me name's Will Miller." He paused slightly before continuing. "Dinners at 1 o'clock. The cook asks that ye send someone up from your compartment with the cans to collect it from the cook-house."

Richard looked at him blankly. Thankfully Mrs O'Loughlin took charge. "Thank ye, Mr Miller. Tell me where to find the cook-house like?"

"Oh sorry, ma'am. Up on deck towards the stern. ye can't miss it." He headed off to the next compartment without waiting for more questions.

"Mr Bryar if ye give me your cans, Kate and I'll go and fetch dinner for us all."

Richard thanked her. Following a quick search through the open chest, he retrieved the cans and handed them to her. In the meantime, he rummaged through the chest for tin bowls, plates and cutlery. Not being sure what they'd need he got them all out. He handed the cutlery to young Richard who had clambered down from the top bunk.

They took themselves and the utensils out to the table and sat on a bench to wait. They didn't have to wait long before Paddy and Honora returned from their sojourn on deck.

"Ah, tis a fine ship. We was speaking with one o' the mates, a Mr Reardon. He says how Captain Weymess wants to weigh anchor at about 3 o'clock, so it shan't be long now."

Paddy looked chilled through but was grinning like a loon. While Richard was dreading the ship leaving Port, Paddy seemed as excited as young Richard at the prospect.

"Did ye see the Captain Mr O'Loughlin?" young Richard asked him excitedly.

"Nay laddie. I expect he's very busy right now."

"Did ye happen to see my wife Paddy? She went off some time ago to see to our eldest daughters and she hasn't returned."

Paddy sat down on the bench opposite Richard and rubbed his hands over his cold face. "Nay. Seems we both be short a wife. Do ye know what's become of mine like?"

"Oh aye. She's gone to fetch dinner for us all. I don't expect she'll be much longer." Richard hoped not anyway as his stomach gave a hungry rumble. He didn't think there was any point going off in search of Mary either. She would return soon enough once she was sure the girls were settled and safe.

"Can we go up on deck Da? Twould be good to see the ship weigh anchor."

Richard looked at his young son. His eager face was alight with joy and curiosity. "Oh aye. After dinner and when your mawther gets back. Don't worry, we'll get up there in time to say goodbye to old England." He ruffled his hair and young Richard grinned happily at him.

Mrs O'Loughlin and her daughter Kate returned a short time later with cans full of pork and pea soup and fresh bread. They had only just finished dishing this out when Mary and Lizzie arrived back. Mary sat down to the bowl of hot soup with gratitude. She had forgotten to take her cloak and was chilled to the bone. She moaned with pleasure as the hot soup began to warm her from the inside out.

"Oh thank ye for getting dinner for us all Mrs O'Loughlin. Twas most kind of ye.'

Mrs O'Loughlin looked up from her bowl of soup. "Ye are most welcome Mrs Bryar. If ye please, ye can call me Catherine. We will be spending a great deal o' time together methinks."

Mary smiled warmly at her. "Thank ye. Please call me Mary."

"So did ye find Alice and Maryann all settled then?" asked Richard between mouthfuls of bread.

"Oh aye. They're on the deck below us at the back of the ship in the single women's section," said Mary. "Somehow they managed to rearrange their accommodation. They be sharing their compartment with the MacDonald sisters."

"Oh...Alice will be awright then." Richard was pleased, it was one less thing he had to worry about. He swallowed the last of his soup and hoped to God that it would stay down. He wasn't feeling sick as such, just unsettled.

"Can we go up on deck now Da?" asked young Richard enthusiastically.

"These dishes need to be washed and put away first," replied his mother. "Ye and Lizzie can take care of them. And take Mr and Mrs O'Loughlin's as well."

Before he could voice the complaints that were clearly on his face

Mary continued. "Go with your sister. There's water and troughs for washing just passed the open hatch. Off ye go now."

Catherine O'Loughlin looked like she was about to interject but changed her mind. She murmured her thanks to young Richard as he took her bowl and spoon. She then indicated to Kate and Honora that they should help as well.

Chapter 8

Lizzie went to fetch Alice and Maryann before they all went up onto the deck. The chilly wind had died down somewhat, although it was still cold enough for Mary to be thankful for her gloves. She took a sideways glance at Richard. He looked a little pale she thought, but there were no telltale signs of seasickness, at least not yet.

The deck was crowded with people. Mary thought everyone on board must have been hanging over the railing. Some were calling to people on the dock while others were waving madly to loved ones they may never see again. Her heart fluttered at the thought. No - she would see Thomas and Jenni again she was sure of it.

She was so glad Richard had taken her to the churchyard in St Hilary to say final goodbyes to the five bearns they'd lost. Four of them had died when they were only months old so they'd never really known them. Philip had been six years old, and the spitting image of his father. A quiet boy, not unlike Thomas in some ways. Mary knew she'd never visit their graves again, but she'd never forget them either. The pain of such a loss never really leaves you; she knew that. She turned her attention back to the present and her heart lifted at the sight of her family. She was more fortunate than some.

They were standing near the bow of the ship where young Richard could get a good view of the towing tugs. There were two of them tethered to the ship with long lines. When the ropes that had tethered the ship to the wharf were removed the ship began to slowly move under the tow of the tugs. The Monsoon slid gracefully passed the other ships moored at the docks. In no time they were well on their way to the Channel.

The ship was taken about two miles outside Southampton Water before the tow lines were dropped and the tugs moved away. Young Richard grabbed his father's arm and pointed as the sails were unfurled and the Blue Peter was raised. The delight and excitement was evident on his young face. Mary didn't think Richard shared his excitement, however, young Richard didn't seem to notice.

They remained on deck until Mary thought she would freeze if she stayed any longer. The breeze freshened as they started the run down the English Channel. The ship started to gently roll and pitch. It wasn't so bad, but she braced her legs to maintain her balance.

Like most of the passengers, the cold eventually compelled them to return to their berth. They enjoyed a supper of fowl and potatoes, but by half-past eight Mary was barely able to keep her eyes open. Before she retired she made sure Lizzie and young Richard were safely tucked into their bunks for the night. Although the roll of the ship was fairly gentle she worried they might fall out. Richard assured her they would be fine, although she wasn't so sure about him. He appeared to be quite pale and clammy and when they finally retired to their own beds he was breathing heavily. She hoped he wouldn't be sick on their clean sheets.

She had trouble getting to sleep in the narrow bed and unfamiliar surroundings. The ship vibrated beneath her and the sounds of creaking timbers made her stomach turn over. The motion of the ship was not at all what she was used to, and she couldn't understand why young bearns liked to be rocked. She certainly didn't. She finally fell asleep due to sheer exhaustion, but it was a sleep full of odd dreams.

Mary awoke in the morning to find that more than half the passengers on board were seasick. She was thankful she was feeling alright, as were Lizzie and young Richard. Richard on the other hand had turned a rather pale shade of green, and he lay in his berth moaning. Catherine O'Loughlin likewise was lying prone in her bed and didn't look much better than Richard. Mary sent Lizzie to find their steward, Mr Miller, to see if he could provide buckets for them both. In the meantime, she went off to find the ship's Doctor.

The ship was heaving something frightful and Mary missed the first step on her way up to the top deck. She was flung sideways and hit her shoulder on the bulkhead. She was glad she had a firm hold of the rail or else she would've ended up flat on her face. Her shoulder hurt but she didn't think she was badly damaged.

"Are ye alright ma'am?" a young man enquired as he grabbed her by the elbow and helped her to stand upright. "Twill take us all some time to get our sea legs. Take 'old of the rail with both hands ma'am."

Mary smiled weakly at him. "Thank ye kindly. Aye twill take some time to get used to this." She grabbed hold of the handrail with both hands and managed to safely climb to the top deck.

She had no idea where she might find the Doctor. Thankfully one of the crew - who introduced himself as Mr Huddy - noticed her bewildered expression and enquired if he could assist her.

"Och aye. The good Doctor has the hospital set up in the forecastle. Just up the front there ma'am ye canna miss it. Go inside and it's on the right-hand side."

Following Mr Huddy's directions, she had no difficulty finding the hospital and was glad the Doctor was there. He was a rather tall gaunt man with mousy brown hair. He was wearing a pair of dark-rimmed spectacles perched on the end of his nose. He looked over the top of these at Mary as she entered.

"I'll be with you in a minute ma'am," he said before turning his attention back to his current patient. "I'll call in on your wife when I do my rounds," he was saying to the nervous young man. "In the meantime, keep her as warm and comfortable as you can. See if the cook can be persuaded to make her some clear broth.

That'll likely cheer her spirits somewhat." He patted the young man kindly on the back before turning his attention to Mary.

"Now ma'am I'm Dr Johnson. How can I assist you?"

"Oh, tis my husband Doctor. He's feeling very poorly with the seasickness, as is our companion Mrs O'Loughlin. I was wondering if ye might have something I could give them to help ease their sickness."

He shook his head slightly and tut-tutted under his breath. "Half the ship's down with it. Of course, it's to be expected." He went over to the sideboard and poured some liquid into a can which he handed to her. "I've been up since before dawn brewing ginger tea, it should help settle their stomachs. Get some dry biscuits from the cook-house as well. They won't be wanting to eat anything else for a few days."

Mary took the can of tea and thanked him.

"I'll check in on your husband when I do my rounds later, and don't worry, I'll bring more tea with me."

Mary headed off to the cook-house where she managed to get some biscuits and then hurried back down below.

"I've given Da and Mrs O'Loughlin a bucket each," Lizzie informed her on her return. She grimaced distastefully. "Did ye find the Doctor Ma?"

"Aye. He's given me some ginger tea. Go get yourself some breakfast Lizzie, I'll take care of them."

"Oh, Mr O'Loughlin has gone to fetch breakfast for all of us. He'll be back dreckly."

Mary nodded before entering the compartment. Richard opened his eyes and smiled grimly at her. The morning was quite chilly but Mary noticed he was sweating profusely. His hair was clinging damply to him and he looked dreadful.

"The Doctor has sent some tea to help settle your stomach," she said pouring him a cup. She lifted his head and held it to his lips, "sip slowly aye."

He managed to drink a good amount of the tea, although he grimaced and coughed in between sips. "What about Catherine? Did ye bring some for her as well?"

"Aye, I did."

Mary poured a cup of the tea for Catherine as well. She didn't seem to be as badly affected as Richard and managed to sit up and take the cup from Mary. "Thank ye, Mary."

She gave them both some dry biscuits as well. Richard only managed to nibble around the edges of his before lying back down with a groan.

The seasickness lasted for well on a week, and by the time Richard was well enough to keep down regular meals Mary was quite exhausted. Thankfully they had smooth sailing through the Bay of Biscay which seemed to settle everyone's stomachs.

Chapter 9

It didn't take them long to fall into the routine of ship life. They were up at 7 o'clock every morning and were required to be dressed and have their compartment swept out before breakfast at eight. Apart from eating, sleeping and washing dishes, there was very little for any of them to do.

They were now off the coast of Spain and every day it was getting hotter and hotter. Richard wiped the sweat from his brow as he searched through the chest for a light cotton shirt and straw hat.

"While ye are searching through there Richard, see if ye canna find me a cotton petticoat. Tis way too hot to wear this flannel one any longer," said Mary waving her bonnet in front of her face to cool herself.

"I'm going up on deck for a walk with Alice and Maryann," said Lizzie poking her head into their compartment. "Do ye want to join us Ma?"

"No, ye run along. I'll wait for your faather." Lizzie was looking hot but Mary thought she had a nice healthy glow about her. "Ask Alice if she can keep an eye out for young Richard. He went off some time ago with William Joyce. I hate to think what they're up to."

"Awright Ma."

After much heavy breathing and swearing under his breath, Richard finally managed to find what he was looking for. He handed Mary her petticoat before stripping off his shirt and putting on the clean light cotton one.

"Ah, that's better. Come, Mary, at least we may get a breeze up on deck," said Ri9chard trying on his straw hat for size. It had been a bit battered before being squashed into the sea chest for a couple of weeks. It was now quite out of shape and lopsided. He grinned at Mary from under the sagging brim and held out his arm to her.

After being below in the hot and stuffy air it was delightful up on deck. The sun was quite hot, but there was a fresh breeze blowing which lifted Richard's shirt from his hot skin and left a nice cool feeling behind. The deck was crowded with passengers. Some were lounging in deck chairs whilst others were promenading up and down.

Richard and Mary managed to find a spot by the railing near the front of the ship.

Much to Mary's delight, several porpoises were swimming alongside, leaping from the water and playing in the waves. "Oh, I wish young Richard was here. He would love them!"

Richard looked around and scanned the ship as far as he could see, but there was no sign of any of his offspring. "He's probably already seen them Mary, or at least he will afore we reach Australia. Come, let's walk and see if we canna find our bearns amongst the crowd."

They joined the many other passengers strolling along the top deck. They were just near the mainmast when Richard noticed two boys up on the quarterdeck near the helm. One was wearing a faded blue shirt and had a mop of dark hair. "That looks like young Richard." Richard pointed towards the helm so that Mary could follow his line of sight. "What's he doing up there?"

Mary squinted to try and get a better look. "He looks like he's steering the ship!" she exclaimed. "Is that Mr Wilcox with him?"

"Aye I think so," replied Richard as they headed off to find out what was going on.

Sure enough, young Richard and his friend William Joyce were steering the ship under the watchful eye of the Second Mate. The two boys each had hold of the wheel, one on either side.

"Now watch the mainsails there," Mr Wilcox was saying to them. "Ye need to keep 'em full o' wind. That's it, lads. Gently does it."

He looked up as Richard and Mary approached the helm. "Good morning to ye Mr Bryar. Mrs Bryar." He greeted them cordially doffing his hat in Mary's direction.

"Da! Me and Willie are steering the ship," young Richard exclaimed excitedly. "Mr Wilcox says as how he'll make sailors of us yet."

"Oh aye," replied Richard somewhat bewildered. "Mr Wilcox are ye sure these boys should be doing that? I don't know if the Captain would be happy about them being up here."

"Oh twill be alright as they're with me Mr Bryar," said Mr Wilcox with a casual air. "Unless ye'd rather he didn't?"

Richard cast a glance at Mary. She didn't seem too concerned and young Richard looked elated standing at the wheel. He appeared to be keeping a watchful eye on the sails and Richard didn't have the heart to say no. Anyway it was certainly better than him being bored and getting into all sorts of trouble.

"No, I don't mind if he learns a thing or two about sailing Mr Wilcox. But if he's being a bother to ye, send him on his way."

"Will do Mr Bryar," replied Mr Wilcox before turning his attention back to his young charges. "Now, do ye see the compass heading there? We need to bring the ship back to starboard and keep it on the right heading."

Young Richard and Willie nodded in unison. "Aye Mr Wilcox," they both replied.

"Gently does it, boys," he said placing a guiding hand on the wheel. He signalled to the watch to trim the sails. They watched as several sailors hauled on the ropes until the sails caught the wind and the ship came around. "That'll do it. Hold steady now."

"Did ye see that Da? Tis how ye sail," said young Richard knowingly as he grinned sideways at his fellow accomplice.

"Aye, so I see. Well done boys. ye make sure ye do as Mr Wilcox tells ye," said Richard trying to keep the amusement out of his voice. "We don't want to be ending up in the West Indies by mistake."

Both young Richard and Willie rolled their eyes at him - as if that would happen under their watch.

Richard and Mary bid farewell to the boys and Mr Wilcox and continued on their stroll, keeping an eye out for any sign of the girls. The day was getting quite hot, and Richard dreaded going back down below. It was going to be so hot and suffocating in the small compartment they shared with the O'Loughlin's. He decided that he might join many of the other passengers tonight and sleep on the forecastle deck.

A number of the single young men had been choosing to sleep on deck for the past few nights, and it seemed like a sensible notion to him. He wasn't sure if it would be prudent for the girls to join him, but surely young Richard and Paddy O'Loughlin would like the idea.

Chapter 10

Breage Cornwall, 2nd January 1857

Thomas looked up as his mother-in-law entered the small sitting room. His heart was thumping wildly and despite the cold, he was sweating profusely. He'd spent the last few hours holding his breath as Jenni laboured to bring their newest bearn into the world.

Her labours had started well enough when her waters broke early this morning. Elizabeth had sent him off to rouse the midwife, Mrs Watkins, who had come at once. He'd been left in charge of Beth and Susan and told to go away. He managed to cook porridge for himself and the two girls, although Beth complained.

"Mamma does nice porridge. Why's it so thick?" She had some held upside down on her spoon peering at it. The porridge refused to fall off; it was stuck to the spoon like glue.

He was about to tell her to stop complaining and just eat it, but looking at the solid pile of cooked oats in his own bowl he changed his mind. God, they might all end with stomach aches if they ate it.

"Come on. Let's go see if Aunt Grace can give us breakfast." He bundled the girls into their warm cloaks and gloves and put on his overcoat and woolly hat. He was glad to escape the house for a few hours. He couldn't bear to stay and not be able to do anything to stop the pain that Jenni would endure. Grace had given them breakfast and he'd stayed for most of the morning helping Nick in the tavern.

He'd left the two girls with Grace and had been pacing the sitting room now for some time. He'd not been able to block out Jenni's groans and had been hoping and praying it would be over soon. Elizabeth smiled at him as she entered and his stomach unclenched at the sight of her.

"Has the bearn come at last?"

"Aye. Ye have a new daughter," said Elizabeth smiling widely at him. "All's well Tom, ye can go and see 'em now."

He quickly hugged her. "Thank ye, and thank God." He went cautiously into the room he shared with Jenni. Mrs Watkins was still there but on seeing Tom bustled out.

"Congratulations Mr Bryar," she said as she hurried past him.

Jenni was sitting up in bed holding a small bundle in her arms. He could see a perfectly shaped head covered in light brown fuzz poking out from the top of the wrapped bundle. He sat on the edge of the bed and leaned over for a closer look at his new daughter. She was beautiful, even with a wrinkled face and red splotches. She had her eyes closed tight and he wondered what colour they might be.

He looked into Jenni's soft grey eyes and kissed her gently. "We have a new daughter. I couldna be more happy Jenni."

She smiled tiredly back at him and then down at their new daughter. "Aye, and a lot of trouble she was. She didna want to come methinks." She sat thoughtfully looking at the tiny bundle for a few moments before turning her eyes to Tom. "I'm that sorry she's not a son for ye Tom."

He didn't hesitate with his reply. "I don't care Jenni. As long as ye and the bearn are fine and well, I don't care." He meant it. While it would be nice to have a son one day, another daughter didn't matter as long as he had Jenni.

They sat together for some time admiring their new offspring. They would only have a few quiet moments of peace before Beth and Susan returned home.

"I thought we might name her Esther Anne," said Jenni looking enquiringly at Tom. 'I know tis not a family name, but I've always liked it."

"Aye. Esther Anne Bryar sounds fine to me," he replied. "Give her to me Jenni and I'll put her in the crib. Ye need to rest." She handed the precious bundle over without argument and settled down under the covers.

Tom carefully placed Esther in her crib and gave Jenni one last look before he left the room. He suspected she was already asleep poor thing.

Chapter 11

The Monsoon, January 1857

Every day they were getting closer to the equator and every day it was getting hotter and hotter. The deck was so scorching during the day that Richard and Mary, like most of the other passengers, were forced to spend the days below deck in the stifling heat. The crew scrubbed their deck and compartment once a week, but there was no escaping the smell of unwashed bodies with so many people crammed in there all day.

Mary woke to the sound of heavy rain. She hoped they might get a cooling breeze with it. Her shift was stuck to her, and where she and Richard were touching was slippery with their joint perspiration. She rolled out of bed, grabbed a clean shift out of the chest, a towel and soap and hoped there was an unoccupied washroom. It was still early, Richard and the children were fast asleep and she didn't see any movement from the O'Loughlin's either. She tiptoed out of the compartment.

On her return, she ran into Mr Miller who was collecting buckets to catch the rainwater.

"As soon as it fines up ye can have a wash day," he informed her cheerily.

Mary looked forward to it. She and Catherine had spent a morning washing a couple of weeks ago, but they'd had to use seawater and their clothes had dried hard and stiff. "Do ye really think we'll catch enough rainwater to wash?"

"Oh aye, Mrs Bryar. Nay doubt," he replied as he took the two buckets she offered him. "Tis quite pouring and likely to rain for some time yet."

Mr Miller was right. It rained the entire day and everyone had to remain below decks in their cramped quarters. Thankfully a fresh breeze came with the rain and it wasn't quite as suffocating as it had been.

The next day dawned bright and sunny once more. Mary gathered the girls together and the clothes for washing. They spent the morning on deck up to their elbows in tubs of clean fresh water washing clothes, and a good deal of themselves as well. The Captain had strung up temporary lines for them to hang the clothes to dry, which in the heat wasn't going to take very long.

They were crossing the equator today and Mr Wilcox told them that it was customary to initiate anyone who hadn't crossed the line before. This was limited to some simple hijinks on the part of the sailors who tried to lure the young ladies close so that they could tie them to the mast. They were also seen with buckets of seawater with which they tried to douse any of the young men who went to close to them. It was all just a bit of fun and most of the passengers were glad of the distraction.

Once south of the equator they picked up the northeast trade winds which took them off the coast of South America. By early February they'd caught the prevailing westerlies and were on their way to the Cape of Good Hope. The weather had cooled down significantly and they were now enjoying beautiful days and were able to sleep at night. The suffocating heat of the tropics was behind them.

Their steward, Mr Miller warned them that before too long it would get very cold, particularly when they reached the Cape. After the stifling heat, Mary didn't

think she'd mind having to wear layers of
clothes to keep warm.

.~.

The Cape of Good Hope
15th February 1857

Richard shivered as he crossed the
deck from the cook-house to the hatch. It
was freezing, and the ship was rolling and
pitching in the heavy waves. The sea was as
dark as the skies overhead which were
threatening to release a torrent at any
minute. He braced his legs in order to stay
upright and to keep the cans full of hot soup
from spilling.

Young Richard was waiting for him
on the top step of the open hatchway and he
handed him one of the cans. "Be careful ye
don't spill it,' Richard cautioned him as he
made to follow him below decks.

"Don't worry Da, I'll not spill it."
He headed off towards their table where
Mary, Lizzie and the O'Loughlin family
were waiting for them to deliver dinner.
Young Richard lurched sideways as the
ship rolled and heaved but he managed to
hold the can steady and didn't spill a drop.

He grinned back over his shoulder at his father.

Richard groaned and rolled his eyes to heaven. He was really getting too smart for his own good. Richard knew he'd have to take a firmer hand with him when they finally got to land.

They ate their dinner with one hand firmly gripping their bowls as the ship heaved and rolled alarmingly. "Apparently we've just rounded the Cape," said Richard. "I was speaking with Mr Huddy while I was waiting in line for our dinner, and he says we should get calmer seas now."

Paddy raised a quizzical eye at him. "Well, I hope he's right. Ye can 'ardly stand up with the ship bucking like a mule."

Mary nodded. "I don't know how we're going to sleep in our beds tonight if it's like this."

The high seas and strong winds prevailed for the rest of the day, but thankfully by the time Richard climbed into bed that night things were a lot calmer. When he got up in the morning it was to find that it had been snowing, and the deck was knee-deep in places. It was perishingly cold and he wished he could've spent the day curled up in bed under the covers.

Over the next few days, they were forced to spend most of their time below decks as the weather was so inclement. It continued to snow and they had several hailstorms, but at least the sea was calmer.

By the end of February however, the wind had deserted them completely and the Monsoon was becalmed. Richard found this more unsettling than when the ship had been heaving and rolling in heavy seas. After a few days of no wind, an eerie quiet seemed to settle over the ship. Instead of the constant sound of creaking timbers, they could hear the sea lapping at the hull. The sails hung limp barely catching a breath of wind. Everyone was on edge and Richard tried to reassure Mary and Lizzie that it wouldn't last long. As the days turned into a week though, even he began to feel the unease of everyone on board, including the Captain.

However, there wasn't anything even the Captain could do about it. All they could do was wait until the wind returned, and Richard fervently prayed that it would be soon. Tempers flared amongst the passengers and children squabbled. One afternoon two of the men from a nearby compartment came to physical blows. Mr Haggerty accused Mr Connor of trying to seduce his wife and punched him in the face. Before anyone could intervene they had taken to each other in earnest. They punched and gouged one another until they ended up rolling about on the deck in a wrestling match. The fight only ended when Paddy and Richard managed to separate them. Neither was badly hurt but spent the rest of the day glaring at one another. Richard thought they may take to one another again, and so he and Paddy were on their guard just in case.

After eight days of being in the doldrums - as the sailors called it - the westerly trade winds returned. It was subtle at first, barely noticeable, and it was only when the ship began to pitch slightly that Richard realised they were once again moving. The relief of everyone on board was palpable.

Chapter 12

They'd been sailing along under steady winds for about a week when they hit stormy weather. Richard was coming across the deck carrying the cans with supper for everyone. He also had provisions for breakfast that the cook had given him.

"Ye may not be able to get up 'ere in the mornin' if this weather gets worse," the cook had said to him.

He was just approaching the mainmast when a huge wave broke over the ship and he was nearly swept off his feet. He managed to wrap one arm around the ladder attached to the mast and hung on for dear life. One of the cans slipped from his grasp and skidded across the deck. He expected to see meat and vegetables spilling out all over the deck, but thankfully the lid stayed on. However, he didn't think there was any way he could retrieve it, at least not yet.

At the same time, the helmsman lost his footing and landed heavily on the deck leaving the wheel unattended. The ship remained on course as the wheel had been chained. A moment later, however, there was a loud crack as the chain snapped. Richard could barely see the wheel with the amount of sea spray, but he thought he could make out sailors running towards the helm. The ship lurched suddenly as it was brought back under control, and Richard lost his grip on the ladder.

He staggered but managed to stay on his feet and lurched awkwardly towards the hatch. Another wave burst over the side and washed him down to the lower deck. Two other passengers landed on top of him as they slid through the hatch as well. Mr Miller pulled them off him and helped him to his feet.

"Are ye alright Mr Bryar? Do ye know if there are any other passengers up on deck?"

Richard shook his head. "Aye, I'm awright thank ye. I don't know if there's anyone else up there or not. I don't think so."

Mr Miller went up to the top step and stuck his head out. It appeared there wasn't anyone else coming as he pulled the hatch closed.

Richard was soaked through as was the deck. So much water had come down the hatchway that several compartments were completely awash. Their inhabitants were trying to move everything to the top bunks where it was dry. He made his way back to his compartment where Mary and the children were sitting at the table looking wide-eyed and scared.

He put the supper can on the table. "I'm sorry I lost one," he said apologetically. "We'll just have to share what we have."

"What's going on up there?" asked Mary. Her eyes looked as big as saucers in her pale face, as she surveyed Richard from head to toe. "Ye are soaked through. Is everything awright?"

The ship pitched and heaved and Richard sat down with a thump beside her. "Well tis awful to be sure, but I'm sure twill be awright."

Catherine O'Loughlin sat down opposite and looked at him doubtfully.

"Ah, tis a bad storm but the Captain knows his job." At least Richard hoped he knew what he was doing. The ship was pitching and rolling something fearful, and several women and children were screaming in fright. Even young Richard looked a trifle scared. "Come let's eat our supper at least."

Paddy agreed wholeheartedly with that suggestion and proceeded to lift the lid on the remaining can and dish out their supper. It was a meagre meal of preserved meat and vegetables shared between the eight of them, but at least they had something to eat.

"A wave came over the side of the ship and I lost my grip on half our supper. I'm ever so sorry I couldna get to it."

Everyone around the table exclaimed that it was alright, they were lucky he made it back with some supper. "Dinna worry Richard, ye did ye best an' in such a fierce storm too," said Paddy spooning the last of his vegetables into his mouth.

Richard was just wondering how much longer the storm would last when there was an almighty crash up on the deck. Water came pouring into the compartments opposite theirs where the bulwark had just been washed away. Mrs Haggerty who was lying down on her bunk at the time screamed in fright as she was doused in freezing water. The compartment was quite flooded and their beds soaked through.

Mary and Catherine immediately went to assist her, and offered to lend her some dry clothes to wear. Their sea chest had been standing open and all their clothes were saturated. Mrs Haggerty was quite hysterical, and it took some time for Mary and Catherine to calm her down.

The storm continued for most of the night and none of them got much sleep. Richard lay awake for hours trying to get comfortable. The ship was pitching frightfully and he was glad he was tall enough to brace himself. He was able to push his feet against the end of the bed and prevent himself from being tossed about too badly. He wondered how young Richard and Lizzie were faring as they wouldn't be able to reach the bottom of their bunks. Mary had herself firmly wedged up against him but he didn't think she was getting any more sleep than he was. At least she wasn't being tossed about.

He must have dozed off sometime in the small hours and awoke in the morning to find the storm had abated. He gave a quiet prayer of thanks for their safe deliverance, and hoped to never go through another experience like that.

After a simple breakfast of cold salted cod, they all went up on deck to survey the damage. The weather was still quite squally and there was rain on the wind. Mary and the girls after assuring themselves that the ship was still in one piece retreated below decks. Richard didn't think it was as bad as it could have been. The ships carpenters were busy repairing the bulwark on the port side of the ship that had been torn off. Some repairs to the cook-house were also underway. It had been hit by a large wave crashing over the main yardarm which completely inundated it. The cook and his assistants had been up to their waists in water until they managed to open the door. The water had rushed out along with many of the cook's pots and pans.

There were only a few minor injuries among the passengers. Mainly sprained ankles and one gentleman had bruised ribs. All in all, they had come through the storm as well as could be expected. With favourable winds, they were now only a week or so from Port Adelaide, and Richard couldn't wait to get there. After nearly three months of being tossed about mercilessly by the sea, he just wanted to feel solid ground beneath his feet.

.~.

The Monsoon docked at Port Adelaide in the early hours of the 17th of

March. It was a cool autumn morning and most of the passengers were up on deck eager for their first glimpse of Adelaide. Richard, Mary and the children were no exception. After a hasty breakfast, they joined the throngs on the main deck.

Mary's first impression of Port Adelaide was that it was a lot like any other port. All she could see were docks and warehouses. In the distance, she thought there were some hills, but otherwise, the countryside appeared to be rather flat. However, this did not dampen her enthusiasm one bit. She was so relieved they had arrived safe and sound and only hoped that Thomas, Jenni and the girls would arrive in the same condition. It was so delightful to think that she would feel solid ground beneath her feet very soon. She couldn't help but smile with the sheer joy of it.

The crew extended the gangway and she could see several gentlemen standing on the dock waiting to come on board. She indicated to them as she turned to Richard. "Do ye think that would be Captain Brewer? The emigration agent that Mr Miller mentioned we should speak with."

"Aye it might be," he replied thoughtfully. "I imagine a lot of people will be wanting to speak with the good Captain. One of the other gentlemen may be able to help us."

"Hmm maybe. But I would prefer to speak with him dreckly. If we are going to entrust your letter for Tom into anyone's hands, it should be his."

Richard nodded. Mary turned back to watch the men board the ship with some satisfaction. She was confident Richard was in agreement with her. They had to speak with Captain Brewer directly no matter how long they had to wait. Mr Miller had informed them that they would have to wait until the Emigration Agent had cleared everyone for landing. They would then be free to leave the ship, but they could remain on board for up to two weeks if they needed to. She hoped it wouldn't be that long.

The Emigration Office cleared the passengers for landing the following day. Richard didn't find an opportunity to speak to Captain Brewer until several days later. Everyone was in such a rush to disembark, and the Emigration Agents had been kept constantly busy answering questions. They were also arranging transport to Adelaide for those who were destitute. Trunks and chests had to be unloaded from the hold as well as from between the decks. Things were generally chaotic for the first few days following their arrival.

On the third day after docking the O'Loughlin family were ready to disembark. Richard and Mary bid them a fond farewell and wished them the best of luck. Following their departure, Mary started to feel quite anxious. She had this rising feeling of panic that was threatening to overwhelm her. Land was so close and yet she was still stuck on the ship.

The following day Captain Brewer approached them to offer whatever help they might need. Richard explained that they were heading for the Burra Burra Mine.

"Well Mr Bryar, I would recommend you take the train to Adelaide. From there you'll be able to take a coach to the Burra Burra."

"Thank ye for the advice," said Richard. "I wonder if I could beg a further favour from you, Captain? Our son Thomas and his family will be arriving on the Sumner in a month or so. Could I possibly send a letter for him care of your office?"

Captain Brewer looked at him thoughtfully. "Well I couldn't guarantee it Mr Bryar, but you would be most welcome to send it into my care. I will do my utmost to see that he gets it."

"Thank ye Captain I am most grateful to ye."

The Captain smiled warmly at him. "Well good luck Mr Bryar and safe travels."

Chapter 13

Onboard The Sumner, Port Adelaide
23rd May 1857

Thomas unfolded the letter and began reading. It was from his father, and he hoped they'd made it safely to Burra Burra.

20 Creek Street, Kooringa
20th April, 1857

Dear Thomas and Jenni,

We have arrived safely in Burra Burra and have found a place to live in Creek Street. We hope this will only be temporary as we look for a proper house to rent. We most earnestly hope and pray that you have had a safe voyage thus far and that this letter finds you all in good health.

The overland trip to Kooringa was exhausting, and we were not able to bring our baggage with us on the coach. I would therefore recommend that you forward your baggage to us by bullock.

Use the money from the sale of our furniture if you find yourself in need.

The road such as it is, will likely be quite wet and boggy by the time you arrive. I would suggest that you take the train to Adelaide, and from there hire a conveyance to bring you the rest of the way.

God speed and safe journey

Your loving father
RB

Tom finished reading the letter and handed it to Jenni. He smiled warmly at Captain Brewer.

"I canna thank ye enough Captain. Tis a great comfort to know that my faather and the rest of my family are safe and well."

"You are most welcome Mr Bryar," he replied. "As you are heading to the Burra Burra Mine as well, I will give you the same advice as I gave your father. Catch the train to Adelaide and book yourself on the coach for the rest of the journey." He looked at Jenni who was holding Esther in her arms and at Susan and Beth, who had hold of her skirts. "It will be a difficult journey with the younguns Mr Bryar, particularly at this time of year. It has been a wet autumn, and winter is nearly upon us. You may be best served by taking your time and waiting for the weather to improve."

"I thank ye for the advice Captain, and I trust that ye know the situation far better than I do," said Tom. "Although I must confess, I'm anxious to be on my way." He put his arm around Jenni's shoulders and drew her close. "As ye say, we'll take the train as far as Adelaide and then assess the situation."

"Very good Mr Bryar. I wish you the best of luck." He bowed his head in Jenni's direction. "Madam."

Jenni smiled wanly as Captain Brewer moved on to the next group of passengers. "I know ye are anxious to get to Burra Burra, but perhaps we should listen to the Captain. I don't like the sounds of a difficult journey with the bearns. And your faather mentioned how exhausting it was as well."

"Aye, but we canna see how it is from here. Once we get to Adelaide we can decide what's best to do," he replied trying to allay her fears. "We'll pack what we need for the next couple of weeks into the portmanteau, and send the rest of our baggage by bullock as Da suggested."

His words hadn't helped one bit and when she looked at him he could see the uncertainty and fear in her eyes. "Don't worry Jenni. I willna let anything happen to ye or the bearns. If it looks too bad we'll wait in Adelaide for the weather to improve. I promise ye."

She still didn't look convinced but agreed with his plan.

Tom had noticed that the adjoining dock was where the ships came in to be loaded with ore from the mines. Just about every day there was a line of bullock drays loaded with ore from the Burra Burra Mine. He hoped one of them might agree to take his baggage to Kooringa. The next morning he headed off to see what he could arrange.

There were a dozen or more bullock drays lined up waiting to unload their ore. Tom thought it would take the best part of the day before they were all unloaded and the ore loaded onto the waiting ships.

He presumed that most, if not all of them would be making the return trip to the Burra Burra mine. Any one of them would possibly agree to carry his baggage. He eyed them speculatively. They were a rough-looking bunch, well-travelled and dirt-stained. He spied one teamster who he thought looked a bit friendlier than the others. He was a tall lanky man with straggly blond hair, but he didn't have the grim look that many of the others had.

He was leaning casually against his dray as Tom approached. "Excuse me," said Tom smiling in what he hoped was a friendly manner. "I wonder if I could have a moment of ye time?"

The man didn't move but looked Tom up and down. "Yeah, whadja want?"

Tom cleared his throat nervously. "Well. I'm wondering if ye are returning to the Burra Burra Mine, and if ye are, would ye be willing to take some baggage for me?"

Tom saw several thoughts flash across the man's face, and he thought he saw a slight gleam in his eye. "Yeah, I'll be headin' back to Burra. What sort of baggage?"

"I've a trunk and two sea chests," replied Tom gaining confidence. "I'd want them delivered to Creek Street in Kooringa."

"Kooringa...hmm," he said thoughtfully. "Well I've a load of veggies to pick up, but I reckon I'd 'ave room for your baggage as ye say."

Much to Tom's relief, they agreed on a price that wasn't too steep. Mr

Hastings, as he later learned, would come by the Sumner later in the day and collect his baggage. He wanted the money upfront and Tom had some reservations about paying him the whole amount. What if he didn't deliver his baggage as agreed?

"I tell ye what Mr Hastings," said Tom trying to find an agreeable solution. "I'll pay ye eight shillings now, and my faather will pay ye an extra four shillings upon delivery. How does that sound to ye?"

Mr Hastings took off his battered hat and scratched his head. "Yeah alright. I understand ye reluctance to pay me the full amount now. Let's shake on it then," he said extending his hand to Tom.

Tom returned to the Sumner feeling very pleased with himself. He'd send a letter with Mr Hastings telling his father about the arrangements, and the amount he was to pay. Once that was done he and Jenni and the girls could finally vacate the ship. He was feeling the best he had in months and couldn't wait to start the journey to Kooringa. He was not only anxious to see the rest of his family, but also the great Burra copper mine. He hoped he'd be working there very soon.

Chapter 14

The steam train from the Port to Adelaide gave Tom and Jenni their first real glimpse of South Australia. The countryside appeared to be gently undulating with low hills in the distance. What trees there were grew quite sparsely and were a dull green colour. Jenni was disappointed they weren't the rich autumn colours like they got back home at this time of year.

It was only a short eight-mile journey into Adelaide and while Susan didn't like the noisy train, Beth was excited with the new experience. As soon as they were settled in the carriage she pressed her face to the window. She squealed with delight when the train started to move and blew its whistle. Esther fell asleep almost immediately and curled up in Tom's arms like a little hedgehog.

Jenni peered out the window as well, eager to get a good look at Adelaide. It was the biggest town she was going to see for some time. Most of the buildings she could see were made of timber but occasionally there was one made out of what looked like round rubbly limestone. As they got closer to the centre of the town there were a lot more two-storey buildings and most of them had verandas. She imagined these would help keep the rain off people as they went about their business.

After what seemed like no time at all the train pulled into the Adelaide Station. It was as far as the train went, but Tom told her they were laying more rails and eventually, it would probably go all the way to Burra Burra. She thought that would be wonderful. The station itself was a lovely brick building with a wide veranda overhanging the station platform.

Tom carefully handed Esther to her so that he could carry the portmanteau. He scooped two-year-old Susan into his arms as well, and told Beth to take hold of her mother's skirts as they disembarked from the train. The train was full of passengers, mainly immigrants from the Sumner like themselves. Everyone was eager to disembark and arrange transport to their final destination. Tom and Jenni were no exception.

They made their way through the crowded station with Tom leading the way. Jenni tried to keep up as best she could. It was rather difficult with so many people and she lost sight of him as he headed out the main doors. Once out on the footpath, she realised he was waiting for her to catch him up.

The street was wide and quite busy with horses and various carts and conveyances. It was all quite bewildering and Jenni didn't know how they were going to arrange transport. There were several conveyances lined up outside the station, but they looked like local carriers. Anyway, they were quickly being filled by eager passengers and their luggage, and Jenni didn't think they had any hope of getting a seat on any of them.

"What are we going to do?"

Tom was looking up and down the street, and Jenni didn't think he had any more idea of what they were going to do than she did. Esther began to wriggle and fuss, so she hoisted her onto her shoulder and whispered soothing words to her.

"Well...I'll go and speak to the Station Master. He will surely know who's running the coach to Burra Burra," he replied. "Wait here." He dropped the portmanteau at Jenni's feet and put Susan down beside her mother. "Stay here with your mawther." No sooner had he put Susan down than he headed off back inside the station.

Jenni grabbed Susan by the hand and drew her closer. "Come on over here with Beth." Jenni wished they'd all gone back inside. While it wasn't freezing, there was a chilly wind blowing and the sky was heavy and overcast. She hoped Tom wouldn't be too long. People bustled past her and one of the drivers was hailing potential customers for the district of Unley and Mitcham. She tried to catch his attention, but she couldn't leave their bag unattended. With the three girls hanging off her it was impossible to move. She sighed and jiggled Esther gently up and down in an attempt to settle her squirming. She wished Tom would hurry up.

He probably wasn't any longer than twenty minutes but it seemed an eternity to Jenni. "Well," she said hopefully when he returned. "I hope ye have arranged something for us?"

"Aye. The station master was very helpful. A Mr Opie runs the mail coach between here and Burra Burra, and I've booked us a seat with him." He picked up their bag and took young Susan by the hand.

"Oh well done Tom," she replied slightly surprised that it had been so easy. "I was afeard we'd be stuck here."

"Well, we will have to stay for a bit. The coach only runs once a week and he was booked out for tomorrow, so we'll have to wait till next Tuesday."

Jenni didn't think a week in Adelaide would be too bad. She'd have a chance to look at the shops, not that she'd be able to buy very much. They only had the one portmanteau, and it was already full with what they thought they might need for the next couple of weeks. Still, it would give them a chance to have a really good look around.

"That's not so bad," said Jenni. "I just hope we can get to Burra Burra before winter sets in."

"So do I," replied Tom. "Come on we canna stand here all day. The station master suggested we stay at the Terminus Hotel over the road. He said they're reasonably priced and clean."

It rained solidly for the next four days and Jenni was disappointed they weren't able to get out and see the town. Instead, they had been confined indoors and by the fourth day, she was nearly going mad. Beth and Susan had done nothing but squabble and irritate one another. Not that she blamed them. There wasn't much for them to do. They had one book between them and a bag of marbles, but they'd had enough of them. She was thankful that Esther was such a good bearn. As long as she was fed and dry she was happy and placid.

She'd sent Tom out shopping to buy some ribbon and beads for the girls to make necklaces. Hopefully, he'd be back soon and they would stop their bickering.

Jenni put Esther down for a nap and decided to take the opportunity to write to her mother. It would be months before she received it, and even longer before she could hope to receive a reply. But writing to her somehow brought her mother closer. She also wanted to let her know they'd arrived safe and they were all well. She would have loved to include a photograph of themselves and the children, but at a cost of eight shillings, it was out of the question.

The following day the rain finally stopped and they were able to get out and have a look around Adelaide. It appeared to be a thriving town, with quite a number of shops and businesses, particularly in Hindley Street. It was the main thoroughfare and although it was quite muddy it was crowded with carts and people. Jenni enjoyed the hustle and bustle but didn't think she'd like to live there. She was far more used to life in a small village and imagined that's what it would be like in Kooringa.

She was anxious about the journey ahead and prayed the weather would stay dry for the next week or so. The sky was cloudy and overcast with a little wintery sunshine poking through. She didn't like their chances of it staying dry for too long.

Chapter 15

Tuesday, 2nd June 1857

The mail coach was due to depart Adelaide at noon and Tom wanted to be sure they were on it. They checked out of the hotel at ten o'clock and had spent the last couple of hours in the waiting room at the station. The day was cool but dry and only a few clouds were scudding across the sky. Tom didn't think there was much chance of rain today at least.

They weren't the only passengers waiting for the mail coach. Two middle-aged men introduced themselves as George and William Martin. They were only going as far as Kapunda, and another young couple from Devon. Tom remembered meeting John and Selina Hooper on board the Sumner. He was also a copper miner and they'd be travelling to Burra Burra as well.

At about a quarter to twelve, a rather stocky well-built man entered the station waiting room. "Good morning to ya ladies and gentlemen," he said doffing his hat and smiling around at them all. "I'm your driver Alex Opie. If ya ready to go then we'll get ya luggage loaded and get underway."

He stood aside and gestured for them to proceed outside. Everyone filed out of the waiting room led by the Martin brothers. Tom picked up their bag and taking Susan by the hand followed them out onto the footpath. Jenni was behind him with Esther in her arms and Beth trotting along beside her. Tom was a little dismayed at the sight of the mail coach. It wasn't a coach at all, but a two-wheeled spring cart without any covering whatsoever. It consisted of three seats and by the looks of it, he and Jenni and the girls would need to squeeze onto one of these. The Martin brothers had already settled themselves upfront with Mr Opie, and John and Selina Hooper took up the middle seat.

"Mr Bryar, your eldest girl could sit between us if ye like? We'll take good care of her," suggested Selina Hooper.

"That is most kind of ye, Mrs Hooper," replied Tom somewhat relieved by the kind offer. "Are ye sure ye will not mind?"

"Not at all. At any rate, I doubt you'd all fit on the one seat."

She was right. "Well I thank ye," he said as he lifted Beth onto the cart and settled her in between the Hooper's. "Now ye be a good girl for Mr and Mrs Hooper. Awright?"

Beth looked solemn but nodded to her father.

Tom then helped Jenni up onto the cart and lifted Susan up to sit beside her. He climbed aboard himself and offered to take Esther. He popped her snugly in under his coat where she was well protected from the chilly wind. She snuggled down for a nap almost immediately. Jenni encompassed Susan under her cloak so that she was as snug and warm as possible. He hoped Beth would be alright. She was wearing a woolly hat and gloves and had a warm cloak on as well, but the cart was open to the elements. Hopefully, she would get some protection from the cold being squeezed in between the Hooper's.

Mr Opie jumped up and settled himself on the front seat between the Martin brothers. He looked back over his shoulder at the rest of his passengers. "Ya right to go then?" Without waiting for a reply he took up the reins and signalled the three horses into motion. The cart lurched forward as they took off up North Terrace.

They were only going at walking speed but in no time at all they had rounded the corner and were heading down Hindley Street and into the bush.

Once they'd cleared the busy streets of Adelaide Mr Opie urged the horses into a trot. The chilly wind whistled around Tom's ears and he tugged his hat further down. He pulled the collar of his coat up around his neck as well for extra warmth. However, the chilly wind was the least of his problems. The road was full of ruts and holes and the cart bounced as it hit each one, jarring his spine with every jolt. He grimaced as he tried to find a more comfortable position. Mud was flying off the horse's hooves as they bounded down the road and Tom was glad he wasn't sitting in the front seat. They must be getting covered in mud and would have no protection from the wind.

They'd been on the road for about an hour and a half when Esther started to complain – it was time for her next feed. She was grizzling and wriggling about under Tom's coat and he tried to rock her gently to soothe her. She was having none of it and started to cry in earnest. There was no way Jenni was going to be able to feed her in the jostling cart. She'd have to wait until they stopped and he had no idea when that might be.

Esther continued to grizzle as he jiggled her gently up and down. He put his little finger in her mouth which kept her quiet for a couple of minutes until she realised there was no milk to be had. She screwed up her face and howled.

Even over the noise of the cart, Jenni heard her youngest crying in distress. She reached into her pocket and took out one of the sugar teats she'd prepared that morning. She nudged Tom and handed it to him. He gave her a look of relief as he took the treat and popped it into Esther's mouth. She quieted immediately, although it wasn't likely to satisfy her for long.

It was mid-afternoon when they came to a stop outside a rather dismal looking house near Smithfield. It was an unpainted slab hut with a sagging tin roof over a wide veranda. It didn't appear to have any windows but rather wooden shutters that could be closed during bad weather. Tom imagined it would be rather dark and dingy inside, not to mention stifling in the summer. A rather lean and sinewy looking man was leaning against the veranda post smoking a pipe. An equally thin, unkept woman was sitting on an upturned box mending a faded flannel shirt. Her dark hair hung limp and greasy down her gaunt face.

Mr Opie jumped down from the coach and greeted them. "Afternoon to ya Jim. How ya do Mrs Penny?" He didn't wait for their replies but turned back to his passengers. "We'll be changing the horses here. Ya might want to stretch ya legs and such. Mrs Penny will likely offer a cup of tea and then we'll be off again."

Tom popped Esther under one arm as he leapt down from the cart. It was so good to stretch his legs and back after being jolted about for the past few hours. He groaned as he stretched. He was sure he had a bruised backside and he wished there was some other way they could get to Burra that didn't involve Mr Opie and his mail coach.

"Mr Opie, is there someplace my wife can take care of the bearn?"

Mr Opie didn't seem to want to know anything about what a baby might need and waved his arm in the direction of the house. "Mrs Penny will likely help ya out," he said dismissively as he began to unhitch the horses.

Tom helped Jenni down from the cart and handed Esther to her before lifting Susan down as well. Beth was already clambering down and Mrs Hooper helped her reach the ground safely. "Can ye get me a dry clout out of the bag Tom?" asked Jenni as she walked over to the house to speak with Mrs Penny.

"Aye. Methinks Susan will need some dry drawers as well," he called to her as he headed around the back of the cart to their portmanteau. He'd noticed that Susan was rather damp when he lifted her from the cart.

Mrs Penny was far more obliging than she'd appeared and invited Jenni into the house so she could feed and change Esther. Susan went to follow her, but Tom took her by the hand and called Beth. "Come on let's see if we canna find the privy."

Susan looked up at him with her big grey eyes. "Me wet Da."

"Aye, I know. Don't worry we'll take care of that."

By the time he returned from finding the privy and taking care of Susan most of the other passengers had gathered on the veranda. Mrs Penny had made a large pot of tea which she placed on a rickety table along with an assortment of odd cups and saucers. She was busy pouring the weak black tea when he arrived and she offered him a cup which he gratefully accepted.

He added a little milk to the tea and took a mouthful. All that could be said for it was that it was hot. Either Mrs Penny had been frugal with the amount of tea she'd put in the pot, or the tea was so stale that it had lost all its pungency. However, he didn't complain or comment. It was hot and he could feel it warming him from the inside out regardless of the flavour.

She offered Beth and Susan a small cup of milk each which they both drank down with gusto. They must have been thirsty poor things. He wondered how much longer Jenni would be. He hoped she'd have time for some warming tea before they had to climb aboard the dreaded spring cart again.

He noticed that George and William Martin were busy trying to brush the mud from their clothes. They had copped the full brunt of it flying off the horse's hooves and their cloaks were splattered from head to foot. George even had some stuck to his face which William was trying to remove for him. Tom didn't think there was much point. they were only halfway to Gawler and by the time they got there, they would likely be caked with it.

"If you folks are ready we'll be underway," said Mr Opie appearing at the front of the house. "Thank ya for ya kind hospitality once again Mrs Penny." He strode over to the waiting cart and climbed aboard, while his passengers gulped down the last of their tea and hurried to follow him.

Tom didn't like to barge into the Penny's house uninvited even though he knew Jenni was inside. "Mrs Penny, could ye please fetch my wife."

She gave him an insolent look but opened the door and called to Jenni. "Time to go missus."

Jenni appeared almost immediately holding a comatose Esther in her arms. "Thank ye for your kindness, Mrs Penny. I'm most grateful to ye."

"Humph," she replied.

Jenni smiled as she carefully laid Esther in Tom's arms. "I'll get the girls into their seats." She kissed her sleeping daughter on the forehead. As she was saying this Mr Hooper was lifting Beth onto the seat. She thanked him as she lifted Susan onto their seat. She climbed up beside her and tucked her in under her cloak once again. She put her arms out to take

Esther but Tom managed to climb up without disturbing his sleeping bundle.

He only just had enough time to settle Esther back under his coat when the cart lurched forward and they were off. Mr Opie urged the horses forward as fast as they would go and the coach bumped and jostled horribly. Tom was regretting having climbed back on board as the coach collided with a fallen log. His backside left the seat as the wheels went over the log and he landed hard back down on his coccyx bone. He winced as pain shot up his back and down his legs. He leaned forward to ease the pressure on his tailbone and groaned as the cart hit another pothole.

Susan was crying and Jenni was doing her best to try and quieten her. Tom wasn't sure if she was hurt or had just been frightened. Jenni wouldn't be able to hear him over the noise of the coach so there wasn't much he could do. Mrs Hooper had her arm around Beth and he hoped she was alright. He didn't think she was crying.

They continued on for another hour or so and Tom fervently hoped they'd arrive in Gawler soon. His back was aching and Esther was a dead weight in his arms which were starting to go numb. No matter how he tried he couldn't get comfortable, and every time he leaned back pain shot through his bruised tailbone. The wind was getting colder and dark clouds were gathering and looking ominous. He wouldn't be surprised if they got some rain before too long, and he worried they'd all catch their death if that happened.

His worst fears were realised a short time later as the heavens opened and it poured. Mr Opie didn't slow the horses and they ploughed on regardless of the rain, splashing along the road and hurling water and mud at the hapless passengers. There was no escaping the wind and rain that chilled Tom to the bone. He had never been more miserable in his life and regretted ever climbing aboard Mr Opie's coach. He was sure Jenni and the girls were just as cold and miserable as he was, but there wasn't anything he could do to reduce his own misery, let alone theirs. At least Esther was snug under his coat and appeared to be dry and warm.

It was late afternoon when they finally arrived in Gawler and the coach pulled up outside the Old Spot Hotel. Tom wasn't sure he could get down from the cart. He was soaked to the skin and freezing cold and his limbs felt like lead. He didn't think he was alone and expected everyone was feeling just as wretched as he was.

Mr Opie appeared to be the only one unaffected by the miserable journey from Adelaide. He jumped down from the coach seemingly oblivious to his passenger's plight. "We'll be staying here o'ernight. I'm sure Mrs Calston will have prepared a nice hot supper for us," he said jovially as he began unloading the luggage from the coach.

The Old Spot Hotel was an impressive two-story cream stone building with a wide balcony running along the second floor. It looked very inviting with swirls of smoke coming out of the chimney. It was the thought of a warm fire and supper that finally got Tom's limbs working and he climbed down from the coach. Jenni got down as well and Tom could see she was shivering all over and he worried she would catch a terrible cold. He handed a squirming Esther to her.

"Go inside Jenni, you're freezing. I'll bring the girls."

She was too weary to argue so simply nodded and headed off towards the main door of the hotel. Mr Hooper kindly lifted Beth down from the cart and placed her on the footpath. She looked so cold and forlorn it broke his heart. He had no way of knowing just how miserable their journey to Burra Burra was going to be. As much as he regretted seeing his eldest daughter so wretched they had no other choice. He sighed as he lifted Susan and held her in his arms. At least she felt warm and dry.

"Come on let's go see if there's a nice warm fire," he said taking Beth by the hand and heading into the hotel after Jenni.

Chapter 16

Kooringa, June 1857

Mary clutched the letter to her bosom and sighed. She'd recognised Tom's writing immediately and was surprised at the tears that sprang to her eyes. She'd been so busy since arriving in Kooringa she hadn't given Thomas, Jenni and the girls much thought. It was only now with news of them in her hands that she realised how much she'd missed them and how hollow she'd been feeling. She felt lighter than she had in months, and couldn't help the wide smile that came across her face.

She was thankful Tom had addressed the letter to both Richard and her. She wouldn't have to wait to read it, not that she thought she'd be able to resist in any case. Without another thought or hesitation, she tore open the envelope.

Old Spot Hotel Gawler
3rd June, 1857

Dear Father and Mother,

I trust this letter finds you both in the best of health. We have arrived at last and Jenni and the bearns are well and in good spirits. I have taken your advice and forwarded our baggage by bullock to you at Kooringa. It will likely arrive afore we do. The arrangement I have made with the driver, Mr Hastings, is that you will pay him four shillings upon delivery. I do hope this will be agreeable with you.

I have arranged a conveyance to Burra Burra, but with the bad weather the roads are impassable and so we find ourselves stranded in Gawler. It is likely we will have to remain here for the next week or so. Mr Opie, who I have engaged to convey us to Kooringa, is hopeful the weather will clear soon.

We are looking forward to seeing you all, and I'm sure you are anxious to assure yourselves of our welfare. Be assured that our accommodation is satisfactory and that Mrs Calston, whose husband runs the establishment, is a fine cook.

Your loving son

Thomas
Ps: Do give our love to Alice, Maryann, Lizzie and young Richard. We hope they are all enjoying the best of health.

She reread the letter several times before folding it and putting it back in the envelope. To think they were so close. If the weather improved they could arrive within the week and her heart fluttered at the thought. There had been so much rain over the last few weeks and the grey leaden sky looked like there was more on the way. Tom was probably right; they'd be stuck in Gawler for at least a week. The roads possibly wouldn't reopen for travellers for another week after that. And that was only if the weather improved. Mary didn't like their chances of that. She sighed and went back inside.

She looked around what was currently their home and dissolved into tears. With the recent influx of migrants, including themselves, there was a shortage of houses in Kooringa. She knew Richard had tried his hardest to get them a cottage to rent but there simply weren't any available. They'd had no choice but to join the many other families who'd taken up residence in one of the dugouts along the creek. It had a dirt front with one small window and an earthen roof over tin. After a few repairs and a new front door, Richard had announced it habitable.

There had been a great flood five or six years back and most of the original owners of the dugouts had abandoned them. The one they'd moved into was quite spacious. It had one living room which included the hearth and kitchen area. There were three smaller rooms at the back that they were using as bedrooms.

It had been dug into the east bank of the Burra Burra Creek and although the earth walls had been whitewashed it was so damp. Mary constantly worried they'd all get consumption. Young Richard had already developed a nasty cough and Mary wasn't convinced that it was only a cold. Doctor Morgan had assured her it was nothing to worry about, but she worried it might develop into bronchitis or worse.

They were using two of the back rooms as bedrooms. One for themselves and one the three girls were sharing. Young Richard was currently sleeping in a hollowed-out alcove near the hearth. They could possibly accommodate Tom and Jenni and the children for a short while. The other room was so small it would barely fit their baggage when it arrived. She thought Richard and Tom could perhaps dig out another room or enlarge one. Mary wasn't too sure if that was even possible.

She wiped the tears from her face with the back of her hand and wiped her nose. Well sometimes a few tears made you feel better she thought. And really, she reminded herself, she had a lot to be grateful for. She would have her family all safe and back together very soon, and the dugout was temporary. She was sure Richard would get them a proper home as soon as he could. If only the Burra Burra Mining Company would sell some land so they could build themselves one. But no, according to Richard they wouldn't let even one acre go.

.~.

Mary was busy in the kitchen baking pasties when Lizzie and young Richard arrived home from school. She was surprised to see them.

"What are ye doing home so early?" she asked as she put the tray of pasties in the oven. "Ye aren't in trouble are ye?" She turned to face her two youngest children as she wiped her hands on her apron. Young Richard looked hot and he was wheezing with every breath.

"Richard was feeling so poorly that Mr Oakford suggested I bring him home," said Lizzie. "He couldna breathe and he was coughing something fierce."

"Aye I knew that cough was getting worse," said Mary annoyed at herself for listening to Doctor Morgan. "Come and sit down Richard, you'll have to breathe some vapours. That'll help."

"I'll be awright Ma. I've just got a headache," he said with a note of complaint in his voice.

He coughed and wheezed and held his head as he sat at the table. Mary bustled about the kitchen and put the kettle on to boil before looking through her small collection of medicinal supplies.

"I thought I had some pine oil but I canna find it," said Mary, more to herself than to anyone in particular. "Lizzie, go down to Birk's Drug Store and see if ye canna buy some pine or eucalyptus oil."

"Aye, of course, Ma. I'll go right away," replied Lizzie looking at Richard with sympathy. "Will he be awright?"

"Oh aye he'll be fine don't worry." Mary gave Lizzie a shilling and she hurried off to the store. Mary just hoped Birk's stocked one or the other of the oils; otherwise, she wasn't sure what else might help.

"What's this letter Ma?" asked Richard eyeing the letter from Tom that was sitting on the table beside him.

"Oh tis a letter from your brother," she exclaimed. "They've arrived and should be here in a week or so. They're only a day away in Gawler but the roads are closed with the bad weather." Mary had her back turned to Richard as she stirred the stew that was simmering away on the back of the stove. She didn't see the look of resentment that passed across his young face.

"Oh. Well, that's good," he replied. "Da will be happy."

"Aye. He'll be very happy when Tom finally gets here," she said. "I know he's been waiting for him to come afore making a bid on a pitch himself."

"I could work with Da down the mine."

"No ye could not," she scoffed at him. "Ye aren't even ten years old yet. Ye knows very well ye canna go until you're twelve."

Richard pulled a disgruntled face at his mother and was about to give her a smart retort but instead began to cough and wheeze. He'd gone quite red in the face and his eyes were watering before he managed to catch his breath.

Mary placed a bowl of steaming water in front of him and handed him a towel to put over his head. "Start breathing that steam. Twill help and when Lizzie gets back I'll add some oil to it. Go on now."

"Awright Ma," he grudgingly obliged her by disappearing under the towel.

Lizzie returned a short while later clutching a small vial of pine oil. "Mr Birk says a poultice of onions and garlic on his chest might help as well," Lizzie informed her screwing up her face. "I canna imagine that would smell very good."

"Well I don't imagine so," replied Mary as she added several drops of oil to the bowl of hot water. "Keep breathing that in Richard. At any rate, I haven't got any garlic."

"Oh," said Lizzie reaching into her pocket. "I forgot Mr Birk sent some for ye." She handed the small pungent bulb to her mother.

By the time Richard arrived home from work young Richard was feeling somewhat better. He was certainly breathing easier even if he did smell quite strongly of garlic and onions. His father screwed up his nose at him and gave him a wide berth.

"Is that really necessary Mary? The whole house reaks."

"Aye, it is. Mr Birk says twill help with the bronchitis. I'd not heard of it afore either, but we'll see," replied Mary as she dished out their supper of stew and potatoes. "Alice and Maryann are working late tonight down at the Hotel. Can ye go and fetch them after supper? I don't like them walking home by themselves after dark."

"Aye of course," replied Richard between mouthfuls of savoury stew.

"Did ye tell Da about the letter that came today?" inquired Lizzie. "Tis so exciting that we'll be seeing Tom and Jenni and the girls soon. And I canna wait to see the new bearn."

"No I haven't had a chance as yet," said Mary giving her daughter a stern look as she handed the letter across to Richard. "They've arrived, safe thank God."

"When Tom gets here can I go down the mine with ye Da?" asked young Richard. "I'm big enough."

"No ye canna. Ye know very well twill be another couple of years afore ye can," replied Richard. He opened the envelope and began reading the letter.

Young Richard gave his father an exasperated look but knew better than to argue.

"As soon as you've finished your supper tis off to bed with ye, Richard," said Mary. "And no more talk of going down the mine. Awright?" She knew he was curious about the mine and wondered whether Richard should take him just to have a look and satisfy that curiosity. It might help him settle down a bit.

By the time Richard finished reading the letter, he had a wide smile on his face. "We can only hope the weather clears and the roads reopen soon. I canna wait to see them all," he said with a sigh. "We have much to be thankful for Mary, and very soon we'll have our family all back together. And as ye say Lizzie, a new bearn as well."

Chapter 17

Gawler, 16th June 1857

Tom lit the candle on the nightstand before gently nudging Jenni awake. "Time to get up Jenni."

It was still dark outside and not much better in their small room. He fumbled about as he searched for another log to put on the fire which had burned down. He heard Jenni stirring behind him, and after locating her pile of clothes put them on the bed for her.

Jenni yawned as she put her feet over the side of the bed. "Tis still dark Tom. It canna be time to get up yet."

"Aye, it is. Mr Opie will be wanting to be on the road by four," he replied as he pulled on his trousers. "If ye want breakfast you'll have to get up now." He didn't have a clean shirt to put on so shrugged into the one he'd been wearing for most of the past week. "Come on I'll lace your stays for ye," he said scooping them up and handing them to her.

They finished getting dressed before waking up the girls. Esther had been fed and changed only an hour or so earlier. She was fast asleep and so they left her there while they went downstairs for breakfast.

Susan was grumpy at being woken up in what she thought, was the middle of the night, but cheered up at the sight of a bowl of hot porridge. Beth was her usual happy self and tucked into breakfast with gusto. Mrs Calston had prepared a hearty breakfast of porridge followed by black pudding and poached eggs.

John and Selina Hooper were already at the table and the Martin brothers joined them a short while later. They had been stranded in Gawler as well and were all anxious to resume their journey. Tom was feeling far more apprehensive about the day ahead. He'd been so miserable by the time they'd arrived in Gawler two weeks ago, that he wouldn't have cared if he'd never seen Mr Opie, or his mail coach again. Thankfully his bruised tailbone was feeling much better, but he wished there was some other way they could get to Kooringa.

Jenni finished her breakfast and sat back with a satisfied sigh. "I'll go and tend to Esther then we'll be ready to go," she said as she pushed her chair back and headed upstairs.

"Would ye like to sit with us on the coach again today?" Mrs Hooper asked Beth.

Beth quickly looked to her father who gave her a small nod and a smile. "Aye thank ye, Mrs Hooper."

"You're most welcome Beth."

Mrs Calston came bustling out of the kitchen with a fresh pot of coffee and two glasses of milk for the girls. "Coffee Mr Martin?" she enquired as she poised to pour the fresh brew into William Martin's cup.

"Why thank ye kindly Mrs Calston. Don't mind if I do."

She poured coffee for the two Martin brothers before serving her other patrons. The Hooper's declined, but Tom held his cup out for another. "Thank ye Mrs Calston. Ye make a fine brew," he said as he added milk to his coffee and took a sip.

"You're most welcome Mr Bryar," she replied as she placed the cups of milk in front of Susan and Beth. "Will Mrs Bryar be wanting more tea do ye think?"

"I don't think she'll have time Mrs Calston."

"Quite right," she said as she gathered up the dirty plates from the table. "Will there be anything else then?" she inquired looking around at her customers.

They all shook their heads and murmured that they were quite full and satisfied.

The door to the dining room popped open and Henry the stable hand stuck his head in. "Coach, coach!" he called.

John and Selina Hooper immediately got up from the table, gathered their luggage and headed for the door. The Martin brothers hadn't quite finished their coffee and appeared to pay no attention to the announcement. Tom told the girls to stay where they were until he got back, and went to fetch Jenni and their portmanteau.

"Are ye right to go?" he inquired as he entered their room.

Jenni looked up as he came in. "Aye. I've given Esther another feed. Hopefully, it will hold her till the first stop."

Tom put on his coat and picked up their bag. "Aye, I hope so too."

They went back downstairs, collected Beth and Susan and prepared to board the dreaded coach. It was still dark outside and the air was frosty with a few wisps of fog clinging to the trees. At least it wasn't raining, and Tom heartily prayed it would stay dry until they reached Kooringa.

He settled Beth in between the Hooper's before helping Jenni and Susan aboard and then climbed up himself. Jenni wrapped her cloak around Susan and he tucked Esther under his coat where she promptly snuggled down cooing to herself.

Mr Opie swivelled in his seat to check they were all seated. "Right ya are then?" He turned his attention back to the front of the coach and at his signal, the horses plunged into the early morning gloom.

The road was fairly dry but mud still flew off the horse's hooves as they hurried down the hill out of Gawler. Tom hung on for dear life. Surely Mr Opie was putting an awful lot of trust in his horses to navigate the narrow road in the dark. The river was at the bottom of the hill and they appeared to be driving straight for it. Tom let out a gasp of horror as the coach swayed and swerved onto the bridge at the last minute. He let out the breath he'd been holding as they safely navigated their way across to the other side.

The road was full of ruts and potholes; Tom thought if it was possibly even rougher than the road from Adelaide. They bounced along for several hours and now and again there was a severe jolt as the coach went into one of the larger ruts. They finally came to a stop in the grey dawn of the morning for the first change of horses. Not at a house, but at a fence where an unhappy-looking man stood with three horses. He was a short stubby sort of man with a grim expression on his face. No doubt he'd been standing there for some time and was probably freezing.

Mr Opie jumped down from the coach. "Morning to ya Charlie. The horses ready to go then?"

Charlie approached the coach and started to unhitch the horses. "Aye." He was a man of few words.

"Ya might want to stretch ya legs a bit while we change the horses," said Mr Opie to his passengers. "Twill only be ten minutes mind."

Tom handed a squirming Esther to Jenni before lifting Susan down. "I don't know if ye will be able to feed Esther here," he said looking around for a likely spot. In the gloomy morning light, all he could see was a flat barren landscape with barely a tree in sight.

Mrs Hooper overheard him. "I'll shield ye, Mrs Bryar," she said removing her cloak She climbed up onto the seat beside Jenni. "I'll hold my cloak up for ye while ye feed the wean," she said smiling at Jenni.

"Oh thank ye, Mrs Hooper, that is most kind of ye," said a relieved Jenni. "I don't think she'd make it till the next stop."

Twenty minutes later they were back on the road and according to Mr Opie, their next stop would be Kapunda. In the morning light, Tom was able to get a good look at the countryside. He was a little dismayed at the flat land that extended for miles in every direction. There were barely any trees or shrubbery. In the far distance, there was a range of mountains, but otherwise, the ground was level with swamps and lagoons.

They continued on for three or four miles when there was a loud crack and the cart tilted upwards as they came to a halt. Tom lurched forward and only just managed to catch himself from toppling sideways from the coach. Jenni was thrown sideways but managed to right herself. She grabbed hold of Susan to prevent her from being flung from the cart.

Pioneers of Burra

Mr Opie leapt down from the coach and went to check the damage. The backband of the lead horse had given way and the shafts had fallen to the ground and snapped.

"All out! All out!" he exclaimed. "We won't be going any further today, tis broken beyond repair." Mr Opie began unhitching the horses and released two of them. "I'm afraid you'll have to walk from here. We're about thirteen miles from Kapunda. I'll ride ahead and send back a conveyance for ya."

Amid groans and grumbling, they all climbed down from the coach.

"Ye cannot be serious Mr Opie. Ye expect us to walk thirteen miles!" said an incredulous William Martin.

"I'm sorry but ya have no choice, Mr Martin. I'll do me best to send back a conveyance for ya."

"Do your best! I have spent two weeks in Gawler at my expense due to your poor coach service, and now you expect me to walk halfway to Kapunda!" he exclaimed indignantly. "I expect recompense, Mr Opie!"

"Mr Opie, my wife and bearns canna possibly walk to Kapunda from here," exclaimed Tom. "There must be a better solution than that!"

Mr Opie loaded the mailbags onto the one remaining horse and then mounted up. "I'm very sorry but tis the best I can do." Without another word, he kicked the horse into action and galloped off down the road.

"Tom he wasna serious, was he?" asked a bewildered Jenni. "Has he truly left us here stranded in the middle of nowhere?"

Tom wrapped his arms around Jenni and hugged her close. "I'm afraid so."

She sat down on the ground and began to sob. "I canna do it, and the bearns canna walk all that way!" Mrs Hooper sat down beside Jenni and assured her she'd help with the children, but she was barely holding back her own tears.

"Well we are in a pitiful state ladies, but we'd best get started if we hope to reach an inn before nightfall," said George Martin matter of factly. "Your youngest girl there won't be able to walk far Mr Bryar. I don't mind carrying our bags and my brother could carry her for a few miles at least."

"Yes that's a sound idea, George," William interjected. "I don't mind a bit Mr Bryar if it will hurry us along." He looked at the morning sky which was thankfully clear of clouds. "At least we are not likely to get rained upon."

"Thank ye kindly Mr Martin, that would be a great help to us," Tom replied as he lifted their bag off the back of the cart. "Come on Jenni. Twill be awright," he said kneeling beside her. "Ye will have to carry Esther and Beth will have to walk, but Mr Martin is right, we must get going."

Amid continuing sobs and grumbling they started on the long walk to Kapunda. The road was still muddy from the recent rains and every step threatened to suck the boots off Tom's feet. It was a dreary walk interspersed with groans from the women, and talk of what the Martin brothers planned to do to Mr Opie when they caught up with him. Tom wouldn't like to be in his shoes.

Beth ploughed on in silence. Tom was proud of her. She wasn't complaining at all, and it was difficult going. William Martin was piggybacking Susan and Tom suspected she'd nodded off. He offered to take Esther from Jenni for a while. He knew she could be a real dead weight and Jenni was having trouble navigating the muddy road. Her skirt was splattered with mud and the hem was caked with it.

She smiled wanly at him as she handed Esther to him. "Thank ye." She stretched her cramped arms and plodded on.

They had been trudging along for a couple of hours or so when they came across a bogged bullock dray. The teamster was sitting under a clump of trees beside a nice warm fire. He told them he'd been there for three days waiting for his partner to return with some extra bullocks. However, he seemed quite unconcerned. His dray was loaded with tea, sugar and tobacco and so he offered them all some refreshment.

They all sat down around his fire and waited for the billy to boil. Tom sat Beth on his knee and hugged her as she warmed herself. "Are ye awright Beth? Will ye be able to walk a bit further?"

She screwed up her young face. "Aye, but the mud is so squishy it wants to take my boots off!"

Tom smiled. He was having the same problem. "Aye, it does."

He couldn't believe the situation they found themselves in. All he could do was hope Mr Opie would find a conveyance and come for them before too long. He wasn't sure how much further Jenni and Beth would be able to walk. He felt like he'd let them down. It was his job to take proper care of his family, and he'd stranded them in the middle of nowhere. They couldn't afford to get separated from the rest of their group either. What if they ran into some blackfellows? He'd heard about them, and while they apparently weren't dangerous he didn't like the idea of meeting them alone and unarmed.

The teamster, Mr Jackson, poured them all a mug of hot sweet tea which went some way to lifting Tom's spirits. However, he was having trouble shaking the feeling of gloom that had settled on him.

After resting by Mr Jackson's fire for half an hour or so they started on their way again. They trudged wearily on for several more miles. Each step was becoming increasingly more difficult, and with aching backs and legs, they came to a halt under a small clump of trees.

"We'll rest here for a bit," said George checking his pocket watch. "I expect if Mr Opie has been successful in getting us another cart he should be coming along very soon."

"That's a mighty big IF," said a grumpy William. "I expect ye may be right though."

Tom gladly sat down under the smallest tree. He popped Esther on his lap and stretched his aching arms. He hoped the Martin's were right. He wasn't too sure how much further he was going to be able to go. It wasn't the walking so much as the load he was carrying. His back and arms were killing him and he knew he couldn't expect Jenni to carry anything. Beth looked exhausted and his heart went out to her.

"Do ye hear that?" said Mrs Hooper jumping to her feet. "I swear I hear a cart coming!"

Both the Martin brothers leapt up and stepped into the middle of the road listening intently. "Yes. Yes I hear it!" exclaimed George. "I think it must be our salvation!"

Sure enough, a few minutes later a cart pulled up in front of them. It wasn't Mr Opie and his mail coach, but what looked to be a farmer in an uncovered wagon pulled by two large draft horses.

He removed his moth-eaten felt hat and grinned widely at them showing a mouthful of half rotting teeth. "Howdy folks. I expect ye be Mr Opie's passengers? He sent me to get ye."

They all heaved a collective sigh of relief. While the wagon was just a tray with low sides, at least it was better than their current circumstance. They put their luggage aboard and then all climb into the back of the wagon. There weren't any seats, and the remnants of the previous cargo were still evident. It smelled of rotting cabbages and cow manure, but no one complained as the driver clicked the horses into a slow gait towards Kapunda.

Chapter 18

It was early evening before they finally arrived in Kapunda. They were battered and bruised from the uncomfortable journey in the back of the wagon. Jenni was weary and exhausted and her limbs felt like lead as she climbed down from the back of the wagon. She'd never felt so worn out and tired in her entire life. She hoped someone had prepared a hot supper for them, if not, then she would just go straight to bed.

There was a warm and inviting glow coming from the North Kapunda Hotel. Jenni took Susan by the hand and headed inside. She was greeted by a rather rotund matronly woman who introduced herself as Mrs Murray, the proprietress of the establishment. She immediately scooped Susan into her arms.

"Och, ye poor wee lass! Come this way ma'am, ye must be exhausted after the day you've had. Mr Opie was beside hi'self when he told us what had happened to ye." She chatted gaily as she led the way through to the dining room. "I've prepared ye a nice hot supper. Sit down. Sit down, it willna be verra long."

Jenni gratefully sank into one of the tall back dining chairs. She wondered if there would be any chance of a bath. She would ask Mrs Murray later. For now, it was just so nice to be enveloped by the warmth of the fire and to sit on a comfortable chair.

Tom and Beth arrived a few minutes later with the Martin brothers and Mr and Mrs Hooper. Esther was asleep in his arms, but Jenni didn't like their chances of her staying that way for long. She would no doubt wake up squawking for her supper before Jenni had a chance to have hers. She sighed. Poor Beth looked beyond exhausted, and Jenni hoped she'd stay awake long enough to eat something. She'd need all her strength.

Mrs Murray came bustling back into the dining room, followed by two young girls carrying large trays laden with dishes. By the wonderful aroma coming from the trays, Jenni was in no doubt Mrs Murray had a very good cook working in her kitchen. Her stomach rumbled at the thought of a delicious supper.

They placed the dishes on the table before them. There were beef pies and roast potatoes, and in another bowl a variety of vegetables. Mrs Murray placed a large jug of cider in the middle of the table and told them all to help themselves.

She was about to leave when she noticed Esther sleeping in Tom's arms. "Och, give me the bairn so ye can eat ye supper in peace."

Without waiting for Tom to reply or hand the child over, she snatched Esther up into her arms and headed out the door. Tom looked after her with a bewildered expression but shrugged at Jenni. What could he do? She raised her eyebrows, but they were both too tired to worry. No doubt Mrs Murray would return their daughter when she started to scream for her supper.

Jenni cut up some pie and potatoes so for Susan and Beth. She hoped they'd stay awake long enough to eat it. They both looked so tired. The first mouthful of pie was delicious. However, by the time Jenni had finished her supper, she was yawning and ready for bed. She sighed as she wondered what Mrs Murray had done with Esther. She didn't have to wonder for very long.

A few minutes later Mrs Murray came back into the dining room carrying a snoring Esther in her arms. Jenni raised a quizzical brow at her, but Mrs Murray just smiled broadly.

"The wee mite's so full she'll no doubt sleep till morn," she said placing Esther in Jenni's arms. "My kitchen hand, Mary, gave the wee lass her supper so you've no need to fash."

Jenni had no idea what she meant by that but thanked her nonetheless. "Ye luggage has been taken up to ye rooms, and Johnny here'll show ye the way," she said as she began clearing the table.

Tom lifted a sleepy Susan into his arms and took Beth by the hand and nodded to Jenni to go first. Jenni got to her feet and followed Johnny upstairs to their room. It was a small but comfortable room with two small trundles under the window. A cot had been brought in for Esther. A warm fire was blazing in the hearth and although the furnishings were more than a bit shabby, it exuded a friendly and cosy atmosphere.

The girls were in bed and asleep in no time, and Tom and Jenni weren't far behind them. The mattress was a bit lumpy, but Jenni couldn't have cared less. Her weary body was just so grateful to be lying down. She drifted off into a dreamless sleep without another thought.

.~.

The following morning Mrs Murray made arrangements for Jenni and the girls to enjoy a hot bath. In the meantime, Tom made enquiries about where he might find Mr Opie. He had no intention of being stranded in Kapunda for any length of time. He was anxious to find out when Mr Opie thought they might continue their journey.

Mrs Murray wasn't entirely sure where he was. She told Tom the local blacksmith and wainwright, old Jimmy Hogan, was the only place in town where Mr Opie would be able to get another coach. His establishment was situated just around the corner on Whittaker Street.

"Ye canna miss it, Mr Bryar," Mrs Murray told him. "O'course I dinna know if Mr Opie will be there. The last thing he said to me was that he was going to see if he could borrow a coach. He didna say where from, and he didna say where he was staying."

Tom thanked her and went off in search of Mr Hogan. It was a chilly morning with a few wisps of fog still hanging about. Thankfully it was dry and the sky was clear. He turned the corner and walked down Crase Street which ran into Whittaker Street. According to Mrs Murray's directions, Jimmy Hogan's shop was just around the corner on the left-hand side. He had no problem finding it.

His shop was an unpainted timber fronted shed with double doors in the middle and windows on either side. Several coach wheels were leaning against the front of the shop along with an assortment of spare parts. A large painted sign was attached to the front of the shop which read J Hogan, Blacksmith and Wainwright.

Tom went inside. It took a few moments for his eyes to adjust to the gloomy interior of the workshop. There was a large forge and anvil on the left-hand side with a variety of smithies tools hanging from the rafters. The rest of the shop was taken up with all sorts of timber, a half-assembled spring cart and woodworking tools of all descriptions. There was another set of large double doors which led out into the yard. It appeared to be filled with a jumble of wagon hitches and wheels. The smell of freshly cut timber was strong in the air, and Tom could see a man, who he presumed was Jimmy Hogan, working on an axle.

"Mr Hogan?" Tom enquired as he made his way over to the man. "I'm wondering if I might have a moment of your time."

Tom realised as soon as the man looked up at him that he couldn't be the old Jimmy Hogan Mrs Murray had described. He was only a young man with sandy coloured hair and a face full of half-grown whiskers. Tom thought he'd be barely eighteen years old, and it'd be a few years yet before he'd grow a beard of any decency. He smiled to himself.

The young man stood up and looked Tom up and down with alert blue eyes. "Aye. But I imagine tis me grandfather you'd be wantin' to see," he replied going back to his work. "Well, e's not 'ere."

"Can ye tell me when he might be back?"

Young Mr Hogan went on with his work like he hadn't heard him. Tom shifted his weight from side to side while he waited. He was beginning to think he hadn't heard him when he finally looked up again.

"Can't say for sure. Maybe later today, maybe not til tomorra."

Tom wasn't getting anywhere. He wasn't even sure Jimmy Hogan would know anything about Mr Opie and his coach. He certainly had no intention of coming back tomorrow only to discover that he'd wasted his time. He cleared his throat and tried again.

"Well, it's just that I was hoping he might know something about Mr Opie and his mail coach which broke down yesterday. Do ye know if Mr Opie has been in to see your grandfather?"

The axle young Mr Hogan had been fitting to the spring cart finally slid into place with a clunk. He stood up and stretched. "Oh aye, that's who e's gone off with," he replied. "They left 'ere at the crack o' dawn this mornin' with a couple o' new shafts to fix the cart." He wiped his hands on his trousers and headed over to the workbench. "Like I say, they might be back later on, or more like tomorra," he said over his shoulder.

Tom sighed with relief. If they managed to fix the cart today then they'd be back on the road to Kooringa tomorrow sometime. Thank goodness. He didn't want any further delays. "Thank ye, Mr Hogan. Ye have been most helpful."

Young Mr Hogan grunted a response, but he'd already dismissed Tom and was completely absorbed in his work once again. Tom left the workshop and headed back to the Hotel to give Jenni the good news.

Chapter 19

Kapunda, 18ᵗʰ June 1857

They spent another night at the North Kapunda Hotel under the care of the motherly Mrs Murray. By the following morning, Jenni was beginning to feel much better about things. The girls had slept well for the last couple of nights and were looking much brighter. Jenni was still sporting several bruises, but they were fading as was the memory of the horror trip from Gawler.

They were enjoying a wonderful breakfast of poached eggs and sausages with freshly brewed coffee when word arrived from Mr Opie. Mrs Murray came bustling into the dining room with a message in hand.

"Well, tis good news from Mr Opie. The coach has been repaired, and he expects to be back on the road at noon," she informed them grinning broadly. "Dinna fash, I'll pack a picnic for ye take on the road."

It was just after noon when Johnny poked his head into the lounge where everyone was waiting. "Coach! Coach!" he called. "Mr Opie be ready for ye all. Ye luggage is a'ready aboard."

John and Selina Hooper led the way outside to the waiting coach. Jenni climbed aboard with some trepidation. There was a chilly wind blowing and the sky was overcast and dull. She prayed they would not get rained on again today. However, she didn't like their chances of staying dry. She tucked Susan in under her cloak and pulled the hood up over her head as she settled herself on the back seat next to Tom. Once again he had Esther snuggled in under his coat, where she was well protected from the cold wind. Beth was sitting with the Hooper's and was also well rugged up against the chill.

Mr Opie climbed up onto the front seat and turned to face his passengers. "All set? We've just got to pick up one more passenger from the Wheatsheaf Inn and then we'll be on our way." He turned his attention back to the horses and clicked them into a slow gait down Main Street.

The Wheatsheaf Hotel was only a couple of miles north of Kapunda on the road to Hamilton. It didn't take long to reach the Inn, but by the time they pulled up out the front of it, Jenni was cramped and stiff with the cold. There wasn't enough room for her to stretch her legs and she sighed as she slumped in her seat. She just couldn't wait to get to Kooringa, and then she wasn't going anywhere ever again on Mr Opie's mail coach.

Mr Opie leapt down from the cart and headed into the hotel to fetch his passenger. He emerged a couple of minutes later carrying a large portmanteau which he hoisted onto the back of the coach. His new passenger, a rather portly middle-aged man with thinning dark hair, was quick on his heels. Jenni thought he looked rather grim and sober, and without even acknowledging them he climbed up onto the front seat. Mr Opie got back on board and signalled the horses forward, and they started trotting down the road towards Hamilton. The cold wind blew around Jenni's ears and she tried to pull her hood forward to stop the chilly breeze. She groaned and pulled Susan closer to keep her warm.

They had barely been back on the road for an hour when it started to drizzle with rain. Jenni hoped they'd be stopping for a change of horses soon. At least they'd be able to get out of the rain for a bit and Esther would need feeding.

They pulled up outside a farmhouse just north of Marrabel for the first change of horses. It was a rather typical looking slab type house with a rickety-looking veranda. Well, Jenni thought to call it a veranda was being very kind. It was just a bit of tin attached to the front of the house with a couple of logs for support. The house had been built flat on the ground and the veranda had a dirt floor rather than a timber one. She suspected the whole house had a dirt floor and grimaced at the thought of trying to keep it clean.

Mr Opie jumped down from the coach. "We'll be changing the horses here, so ya'll have time to stretch yourselves and have a bite to eat," he said as he headed for the front door of the house. "Mrs Murray packed us some sandwiches, they're in the back there."

They all climbed down from the cart and headed for the veranda which provided some shelter from the drizzling rain. There were a couple of old wicker chairs and Jenni sank into one of them with Esther in her arms. Mrs Hooper was such a godsend. She smiled warmly at Jenni as she removed her cloak and held it up around her while she fed Esther.

Jenni could see that Selina Hooper was shivering with the chill of removing her only piece of warm clothing. "Tom. Give Mrs Hooper your coat, she's freezing."

"Oh no I'll be fine," she protested.

"Nonsense," said Tom as he removed his coat and wrapped it around her shoulders. "Tis the least I can do after your kindness, Mrs Hooper."

She blushed slightly but accepted his coat with thanks.

With the horses changed and everyone having enjoyed Mrs Murray's packed luncheon they all climbed aboard the coach once more. The drizzling rain had eased but the wind was still blowing a cold chill in their direction. Jenni settled herself back down and pulled her hood over her head. The coach lurched forward and they were off trotting down the rutted road. If the weather held they would reach Black Springs by nightfall, and then tomorrow they would be in Kooringa. She wondered how Richard and Mary and the children were settling into life there.

The letter Richard had left for Tom and herself had been a bit cryptic now that she thought about it. It had mentioned they had a place to live but that it wasn't a proper house. Her heart sank as it dawned on her that they might be living under canvas. What else could it mean? She most certainly didn't fancy spending a cold winter in a tent with three young bearns! She gave Tom a sideways look and gazed at Beth sitting straight-backed on the seat in front of her. What had they brought their family to?

They'd come all this way for opportunities for Tom and a better life for their children. All Jenni could see at the moment was hardship in an uncivilised world. She could feel the panic rising in her chest and tears pricked the back of her eyes. She blinked rapidly to try and stop the feeling from overwhelming her. They had overcome so much already to get here, and she hoped they had not endured those hardships for nothing.

She thought of her mother and brother back home in Cornwall - and had never longed to see them so much as she did right now. She would likely never see them again and the tears that she had been holding at bay ran freely. She was glad no one would notice as the cold wind blew them from her face almost as soon as they landed.

The sun was setting when they arrived in Black Springs and Mr Opie pulled up out the front of the Emu Hotel. If Jenni hadn't been feeling so weary she would have been utterly dismayed at the sight of it. The Emu Hotel was a rough slab single-story building. There were four bullock drays parked to one side and raucous voices were coming from inside. She didn't like their chances of getting a restful night sleep. She groaned as she climbed down from the coach and headed inside.

Chapter 20

Kooringa, 19th June 1857

It was only a short walk from home to the Burra Hotel where Alice and Maryann were both working. Alice was one of the two domestic maids employed by the hotel and Maryann was a cook's assistant. Sometimes, like today, their shifts coincided and they went to work together and would walk home together in the evenings. Maryann didn't like the fact that their father would come and walk them home if it was after dark. Alice on the other hand was far more forgiving of their mother's overprotective nature.

The Hotel was popular with the local miners and travellers alike and had been fully booked of late with many visitors to the mines. Alice had been kept busy changing beds and cleaning rooms and had been working extra hours for the past week or more. Mrs Barker was a fair and reasonable employer and had promised Alice a day off as soon as things quietened down. Alice hoped that would be soon as she took another load of sheets out to the washhouse.

She was on her way back to make up fresh beds when she ran into Mrs Barker. "Oh Alice, just the person I wanted to see," she said putting a motherly arm around her shoulders. "I've just received news that the mail coach will be arriving later this afternoon. We'll need to have at least three rooms ready for Mr Opie and his passengers."

"Of course Mrs Barker," she replied. Inwardly she groaned at the added strain of more overnight guests. "We have two rooms free but I canna think how we can accommodate three."

Mrs Barker put her index finger to her chin as she often did when she was thinking. "Has Mr Morgan not checked out? His room should be free."

This was not Alice's area of responsibility but she generally knew when customers had vacated their rooms. However, she was drawing a blank. "I don't know, Mrs Barker, but I can check."

"Do that Alice. I think you'll find his room is available. We'll need it changed and freshened up before the coach arrives."

"Aye Mrs Barker," she replied as she hurried off to check out the availability of Mr Morgan's room. She would need to hurry if they were going to have the rooms ready on time. Where was Louisa? Now that she thought about it she hadn't seen her fellow maid in some time.

They generally divided the work evenly between the two of them. However, Louisa had recently fallen in love with one of the stable hands and was never where Alice needed her to be. As if she wasn't busy enough, now she would need to track her down if she had any hope of having the rooms ready on time. She groaned and headed out the back through the kitchen in the direction of the stables.

Even before she reached the stable yard she could hear Louisa's high pitched laughter coming from the stables.

"Louisa! Louisa!" She called as she picked up her skirts and hurried down the path.

Louisa appeared at the open stable door almost immediately. "Coming Alice," she called back as she came along the path to meet her. "I'm sorry I lost track o' the time." She blushed.

Alice smiled at her. It wasn't her problem if Louisa was distracted and not doing her work, but Mrs Barker would most certainly be displeased if she knew.

"Tis awright, but we have to get three rooms made up afore the coach gets here. I need your help or we'll never make it," she said as they headed back inside. "One room is ready to be made up but the other two need changing and cleaning. Ye start making up that room and I'll strip the beds in the other two."

Louisa nodded in agreement and they set to work. As Alice was dropping off the final load of sheets in the washhouse she was going over in her mind what Mrs Barker had said about Mr Opie's coach arriving. She stopped in the middle of the path as it suddenly dawned on her - Tom had written that he'd hired Mr Opie to convey them to Kooringa. Oh my God! Tom and Jenni and girls would be arriving today! It had to be. She could feel the excitement of seeing the rest of her family again surging through her. She had to tell her mother. She'd been so melancholy since coming to Kooringa and Alice thought this news would cheer her up immensely.

Alice could barely contain her excitement as they finished preparing the rooms. "Thank ye for your help, Louisa. Do ye mind if I leave the parlour to ye? I want to ask Mrs Barker if I can fetch my mawther," she said. "She'll want to be here when my brother and his family arrive. Oh, I canna wait!"

"O' course Alice," she said with a smile. "After all, ye have been ever so kind in not saying anything to Mrs Barker about me and Walter."

"Ye know I wouldn't," said Alice looking appalled at the notion. "Tis none of my affair, or anyone else's for that matter." She gave Louisa a quick hug. "But, Mrs Barker is another matter entirely and I wouldna tell her."

She left Louisa to tidy and get the front parlour ready for their guests and went to find Mrs Barker. Thankfully she was never very hard to find. She was constantly on the move checking that everything was in order and making final little adjustments. Mrs Barker liked the Hotel to be ready to deal with just about anything at any given moment. Alice found her in the main dining room where she was checking the table settings.

"The rooms are all ready for the coach arriving, and Louisa is seeing to the front parlour," Alice informed her. "I wonder if I could beg a favour, Mrs Barker?"

Mrs Barker looked up from her inspection of the table cloths and smiled warmly at Alice. "Excellent work Alice. Now, what can I do for you?"

"Well, tis only that I think my brother and his family will be arriving on the coach this afternoon. I wondered if I might go and fetch my mawther so she could be here to greet them?" she blurted. "We haven't seen them since afore Christmas."

Mrs Barker raised her eyebrows in surprise. "You mean the rest of your family will be arriving from Cornwall today? On Mr Opie's coach?"

"Aye, I think so."

"Well of course. Go and fetch your mother. And when they arrive you and Maryann take the rest of the day to yourselves." Mrs Barker smiled broadly at her. "Why you must be so excited at the thought of seeing them again after so long...Go, Alice." She swished her hands in Alice's direction. "Go on now."

"Thank ye, Mrs Barker," she said as she turned on her heel and left the dining room. It was only a few blocks to walk home, but she was anxious to get her mother back to the hotel in time. She wrapped her cloak around herself as she hurried down the street towards home. It was a chilly afternoon but there was a bit of pale wintery sun peeking through the clouds. By the time she reached Creek Street, she was just about running and feeling quite warm. She slowed her pace to a more sedate walk and tried to catch her breath as she neared the house.

"Ma," she called as she went into their humble dugout. She agreed with her mother regarding their current accommodation, and couldn't wait until they found a proper house. She shivered, but not from the cold.

Mary was sitting by the window, which was the only source of natural light, with a basketful of mending at her feet. She looked up from her sewing surprised to see her eldest daughter at this hour.

"Did Mrs Barker give ye some time off? Oh, she is so good to ye."

'No. Well aye, she's going to give me and Maryann some time off. But not now," replied Alice. "I've come to take ye back to the hotel with me. Mrs Barker says Mr Opie's coach is coming this afternoon. Tom and Jenni should be on it. Tis so exciting I canna wait!"

Her mother's face was blank for a moment. Then Alice's words all seemed to make sense to her and she leapt to her feet. "What! Today! Are ye sure Alice?"

"Well I'm not certain, no, but I think so. Tom's letter said they would be coming with Mr Opie. Didn't it?"

Mary had already crossed the room and was pulling Tom's letter from its envelope. She quickly scanned it and Alice could see the joy starting to spread across her mother's face. "Aye. I think ye be right Alice." She looked at her and tears started to fall down her cheeks.

Alice quickly scooped her into her arms and hugged her close. "I know ye haven't been happy here Ma, but we'll all be together again."

Mary wiped the tears away with the back of her hand. "I know, and I'm just that happy. Everything will be awright now. I know it."

She hugged her daughter back. "Write a quick note for Lizzie, young Richard and your faather. Tell them to come to the hotel. I'll go and tidy up and then we can go."

Alice nodded and immediately set to writing a note for the rest of the family. Her heart felt lighter than it had in weeks. She was so just glad to see her mother smile again. Everything would be alright now, and she couldn't help the wide grin that spread across her face.

Mary quickly changed her dress and pinned her unruly hair firmly under her cap. She came back into the main room of the house just as Alice was putting the finished note on the table.

"All set?" enquired Mary.

"Aye. We'll need to hurry though if we hope to get back afore the coach comes," replied Alice opening the front door.

Chapter 21

Lizzie was surprised to find the front door to their dugout locked. She raised a pair of quizzical eyebrows at young Richard, who simply shrugged his shoulders at her. She reached into her bag and retrieved the key and unlocked the door.

"Ma?" she called as they went inside. There was no reply. "Well, that's odd."

Richard didn't seem remotely concerned about not finding his mother at home. "She probably lost track of the time. I bet she's over at Mrs Sampson's having tea," he replied.

Lizzie thought that was most unlikely. Her mother was always here when they got home from school. "I don't think so." She was on her way to check to see if she was unwell and having a lie down when she noticed the note propped up on the table. She picked it up and unfolded it. "She's left us a note," said Lizzie reading the short message.

"Oh my goodness!" she exclaimed turning to Richard. "You'll never guess. Tom and Jenni are arriving today and Ma's gone to meet them at the hotel. She wants us to meet her there."

Young Richard screwed up his face in distaste. "Ye can go if ye wants to, but I'm not going." He dropped his school bag in the corner and slumped down on one of the kitchen chairs.

Lizzie looked at him incredulously. "What's a matter with ye? Tis Tom and Jenni and the bearns. Don't ye want to see them?"

He shrugged his young shoulders and frowned at her. "Not really...Well, I would like to see Jenni and the bearns."

Lizzie looked at him perplexed. What had gotten into him she didn't know. If their mother had said to meet her at the hotel then that's exactly what they were going to do. "Well, it doesna matter what ye wants, you're coming to the hotel with me."

"No I'm not," he replied belligerently. "And ye canna make me. I'll wait for Da to come."

Lizzie didn't understand boys, and certainly not younger brothers. "Well I canna leave ye here by yourself, so you'll just have to come with me," she replied matter of factly. "Come on."

"No. I already told ye I'm not going."

They continued to argue back and forth until Lizzie realised she wasn't getting anywhere. She couldn't leave him by himself, her mother would be furious. She had no choice but to sit and wait for their father to get home. However, she wasn't prepared to let him off completely. She continued in her efforts to pry it out of him. What was his problem?

.~.

Before Richard even reached home he could hear Lizzie and young Richards raised voices. It sounded like they were yelling at one another at the top of their voices. What was going on? He stormed into the house and was greeted by two startled angry faces.

"What the devil is going on in here? I can hear ye halfway down the street," he said scowling at them. "Where's your mawther?"

Lizzie found her voice first. "She's gone to the hotel to meet the coach. Tom and Jenni are coming on it today," she informed her father. "Ma left us a note telling us to go and meet her there but Richard wouldna go." She stared at her brother accusingly. "He doesna want to see Tom."

"What? What's this then?" said Richard turning his scowl on his youngest. "Ye are bickering with your sister because of Tom? What's he got to do with it?"

"Lizzie's got it all wrong Da," he said glaring at his sister. "I just wanted to wait for ye."

Richard was perplexed but didn't have time to work it out right now. He was sure there was some truth in there somewhere, but what this had to do with Tom he had no idea. He had to agree with young Richard on that point, Lizzie must have misunderstood.

"Well if your mawther said to meet her at the hotel that's exactly what we'll do," he said. "Ye two will sit here quietly and wait while I get changed outta these dirty work clothes." He gave them one final scowl. "And I never want to hear ye two yelling at one another like that again. Do ye hear me?"

They both looked somewhat shamefaced and murmured that they wouldn't do that again. Richard went through to the backroom that he shared with Mary to change out of his work clothes. He should have been angrier at Lizzie and Richard, but his displeasure had evaporated with the news that Tom was arriving today.

His timing couldn't be better. It was only about a week until the next survey day and Richard intended to bid for his own pitch. Two other miners had agreed to join his pare, and Tom would make four. Not only that, he could use Tom's help to select a few pitches to bid on. He already had his eye on a couple, but he knew the bidding would be fierce. There would be well over fifty pares bidding for the tribute work, but he was confident they could get a good pitch. He smiled to himself as he headed back out to the front parlour. Oh yes, things would definitely be improving now. And if he could get a proper house even Mary would be happy.

"Come on ye two, let's go meet your brother and his family," said Richard to his two disgruntled children. They were still glaring at one another from across the table. "Tis time to put your argument aside, and apologise to one another."

They begrudgingly obliged by saying they were sorry, however, Richard wasn't under any false impression that they'd meant it. At least they stopped scowling at one another as they headed out the door. He sighed as he followed them. Perhaps by the time they reached the hotel, they would be in a more civilised mood.

.~.

Jenni was eager for her first look at Kooringa. This was going to be home for the foreseeable future, and she was hoping it would bear some resemblance to the villages back home. She was sadly disappointed.

As the coach made its way along the wide muddy streets only one word came to mind to describe the place. Shabby. It wasn't just that the houses looked shabby and unkept either. Every so often there were piles of rubbish which had just been left lying about. Jenni grimaced. Why on earth the people here didn't take better care she didn't know. For the most part, they were her countrymen and women, and they certainly didn't keep their homes like this back in Cornwall.

After months at sea and the exhausting trip from Adelaide, she'd pinned all her hopes on Kooringa being a haven for them. It was not like she'd imagined it at all, and she knew they'd agreed to remain here for the next two years. In reality, she just wanted to turn around and go home. How was she going to make the best of this she didn't know. The only ray of hope was the thought of being reunited with Tom's family. She was looking forward to seeing them.

The coach rounded the final corner and came to a halt outside the Burra Hotel. It was a long brick building with the usual veranda that was so typical. Jenni shook Susan gently to wake her. She'd fallen asleep some time back and had been leaning heavily on her mother. She gave a small cry at being woken so rudely, but quickly blinked and looked about.

Tom handed a squirming Esther to Jenni before leaping down from the coach and scooping Susan into his arms. Mrs Hooper helped Beth down the last step, and she grinned up at her mother.

"We're here!" she announced. "Where's Grammer?"

"Well she's probably at home," replied Jenni. "She doesna know we're coming today."

"Oh," said a slightly crestfallen Beth.

"Here, take your sister by the hand and wait here," said Tom popping Susan down next to Beth. "I'll get our bag and your mawther, and then we'll go and find Grammer. Awright?"

"Oh aye," said Beth clapping her hands together in glee. "And Granfer, we mustna forget Granfer."

"Don't worry, we willna forget Granfer," he replied as he helped Jenni down from the coach.

Mrs Hooper stepped forward to speak with Jenni. "Well, it looks like we part company here," she said. "I wish ye the best of luck Mrs Bryar." She bent down to speak to Beth as well, "goodbye sweetheart."

Jenni smiled warmly at her. "I thank ye, Mrs Hooper. ye have been most kind to me and my bearns. I hope all goes well for ye as well."

Selina Hooper smiled a little grimly. "Aye, we can only hope."

Mr Opie reappeared from around the front of the coach. "Ladies," he said doffing his hat in Selina and Jenni's direction. "I've booked ya into the Burra Hotel for the night. The proprietor, Mr Barker and his good wife are expecting ya and will no doubt have everything in preparation for your arrival. I wish ya the best of luck."

They both murmured their thanks to him. Jenni was sure Selina Hooper, like herself, was glad to see the back of Mr Opie. However, she had to concede she was grateful he'd made some arrangements for them. She still wasn't too sure what Tom's father had meant by finding a proper house to rent. It was comforting to think that at least tonight she would sleep in a proper bed with a roof over her head.

Esther brought her quickly back to her current situation as she started to cry in earnest. Jenni popped her over her shoulder and patted her back, which only quietened her for a moment. She was hungry and in dire need of having her clout changed.

"I need to tend to Esther," Jenni said turning to Tom. "I'll go on ahead."

"Aye. Don't worry I'll take care of the girls, and then we'll come and find ye."

Jenni opened the door and stepped inside the Burra Hotel. It was not at all like she'd expected. The entrance hall was immense and well furnished. Numerous rooms led off from the main hall and an impressive fireplace at one end was blazing. However, she only had a moment to take it all in before Mary, Alice and Maryann swooped on her amid cries of delight. Esther let out a squawk of alarm as she was squeezed in the hug of women. She then quickly resumed her howling with even greater enthusiasm. Jenni did her best to quieten her, but she was having none of it.

They were all talking at once, and it was all quite chaotic for the next few minutes until finally, Alice made herself heard above the ruckus.

"Come with me, Jenni. I'll find ye somewhere quiet where ye can take care of the bearn," she said as she began to guide Jenni down the hall. "Ma, why don't ye and Maryann go outside and find Tom and the girls. They will be so glad to see ye."

Jenni followed Alice down the hall and into a small unoccupied parlour. There was a small fire burning and several comfortable chairs. Jenni removed her cloak and sank into one of the chairs by the fire.

Alice closed the door behind them. "Ye willna be disturbed in here," she said smiling at Jenni. "I canna believe ye are here at last. We have all been so anxious that ye would get here afore winter settled in."

Jenni put Esther on her breast where she settled down to suckling immediately.

Jenni sighed. "We are just so glad to finally be here. As ye know, tis a dreadful journey from Adelaide. I never want to do that again!"

"Oh aye. I canna imagine how ye have done it with three bearns," said Alice earnestly. "Twas bad enough for us. We have much to be thankful for though, including your new bearn. What's her name?"

"Esther," replied Jenni. "I know tis not a family name, but it suits her."

"Tis a fine name."

The two of them chatted away amiably while Esther had her supper. Alice explained how she and Maryann were both working at the Burra Hotel, and what a fine establishment it was. She told Jenni how happy her father was with the mine, and that he would be beside himself now Tom had arrived. She avoided any mention of the dugout. Jenni would find out soon enough. Once Esther had been attended to they went and joined the rest of the family.

Their excited voices could be heard coming from the front parlour. Richard, Lizzie and young Richard had arrived, and for the first time in more than six months, the entire Bryar family were together again. Esther was passed around for everyone to admire, and Beth and Susan argued over who should be sitting on Grammer's knee.

Jenni sighed contentedly. She hadn't realised how much she'd been missing the warmth of family, and the security that came with it. She looked around at them all and her heart squeezed at the thought of her own mother and brother back in Cornwall. Would it all be worth it if she never saw them again? She hoped so.

Chapter 22

Tom and Jenni were anxious to settle into their new abode, and Tom was eager to see the great Burra Burra Mine. Mary was worried that one look at the dugout and they would both want to turn around and go straight back to Cornwall.

"Ye are both exhausted, why not stay here the night and come by in the morning," Richard suggested. "Your baggage is safe and sound and waiting for ye. There is naught that will not keep until the morrow."

Mary sided with Richard in convincing them they should get a good nights rest and come by the house in the morning. "We didna know ye were coming today until ye were almost here," added Mary. "Come by in the morning, twill give us a bit more time to get everything ready for ye."

One good look at his weary wife had decided Tom. "Aye, I think ye are both right. We'll have supper and stay here tonight," said Tom putting his arm around Jenni. "Tomorrow will be soon enough to settle in."

Mary breathed a massive sigh of relief. Not that the dugout was going to be any better tomorrow, but perhaps it would not seem quite so bad if they were well-rested before they saw it.

Richard and young Richard had spent most evenings digging out the small back room. They had enlarged it quite a bit, but Mary doubted they'd fit in enough beds for Tom, Jenni and the three girls. Young Richard was still sleeping in the alcove near the hearth, and Richard had suggested they dig out a couple more for Beth and Susan.

Mary didn't like the idea at all, and for the umpteenth time had asked Richard when they might get a proper house. "I enquired again last week. There are none available Mary," Richard replied patiently. "Captain Roach assures me that as soon as one becomes available he'll let me know."

Mary had fretted all night and cried until Richard finally agreed to go to the Burra Hotel early the following morning and explain the dugout to Tom.

Mary knew if she were Jenni she would want to turn around and go straight back home. They still had two months of winter to get through and she worried that the children would get sick in the damp dugout. She kept the fire burning day and night but there was still a dampness about the place. She sighed as she looked around the house.

The walls had been whitewashed but the floor was just compacted earth. Alice had made a couple of rag rugs which had made the parlour feel a little cosier, but it was hard to disguise the fact that they were living underground. The menfolk didn't seem to mind this so much, but Mary knew her daughters shared her distaste of their current home. She prayed they would get into a cottage soon.

.~.

Richard wasn't too sure how he was going to get Tom alone to discuss the dugout, but was he feeling fairly confident as he approached the Burra Hotel. He went inside and was pleased to find Tom sitting by himself in the dining room. He looked up with surprise at seeing his father so early.

"Good morning Da," he said smiling at him. "I didna expect to see ye quite so early. Jenni and the bearns are still abed."

Richard helped himself to a cup of coffee before sitting down opposite Tom. "Oh that's awright. I wanted to speak with ye alone at any rate," he replied. "Your mawther is worried about the house. We haven't been able to rent a proper house as yet. There's none to be had."

"Aye. I remember ye mentioning it in your letter," replied Tom giving his father a sidewise glance. "Jenni was worried that ye might be living in a tent, but I assured her that was not likely. Mawther wouldna put up with that".

Richard grimaced. "Aye, ye be right about that...but...well the thing is we've had to take whatever we could get." He took a sip of his coffee. It was good coffee and he could feel it warming him, and while something stronger would've helped, he smiled at Tom and continued.

"The thing is, in the early days there was an even bigger housing shortage and a lot of people dug out homes along the creek bank. They were mostly abandoned five or six years back after a great flood came through." He paused and took another gulp of his coffee. "Anyway, we fixed one of them up and that's where we're living at the moment. For the most part, it's quite awright, of course, your mawther isn't happy about it, and I'm doing my best to get us a house to rent. The thing is, the Mine owns all the land and the houses and they haven't built enough of them." He shrugged his shoulders. "I'm sorry we haven't got anywhere better for ye and your family Tom, and your mawther is ever so afeared that Jenni willna want to stay."

Tom was inclined to agree with his mother as he struggled to imagine what the house might look like. "So it's dug into the earth? Into the creek bank? It doesna leak?"

"No. It has a tin roof covered in earth, but no it doesna leak. Tis a tad damp at times and your mawther keeps the fire burning day and night," replied Richard draining the last of his coffee. "Young Richard's been helping me dig out a bigger room for ye and Jenni, but it will need a bit more work. Of course, twill only be temporary, but do ye think Jenni will be awright about it?"

On the one hand, Tom thought Jenni was just so happy that the long journey from Cornwall was finally over that she wouldn't care. She was so exhausted from the last couple of weeks on the road, but he doubted even that would be enough for her to overlook living in a dugout. He sighed.

"I don't know Da," he finally replied. He wasn't even too sure how he felt about living underground, and he was a miner. "There's only one way to find out.

One thing I do know about Jenni, she will try to make the best of it. At least I hope so."

"Aye, well so do I," said Richard nodding. "At any rate, I thought we might leave it up to the womenfolk to break the news to Jenni and get her and the bearns settled in." He rose from his chair and poured another cup of coffee. "In the meantime, I thought you and I could go and check out a few pitches. Survey day is naught but a week away, and now that you're here I intend to bid on me own pitch."

Tom drained the last of his coffee and grinned broadly at his father. "I thought you'd never ask. I have been most anxious to see this great Burra Mine. Is it as good as they say?"

"Yes and no," replied Richard taking a large mouthful of coffee. "Philip Downing was right about the ore being in easy reach, but it costs more to get at it." He smiled warmly at his son. "Oh I think you'll like it well enough Tom, and I'm sure we can make a good profit if we bid well."

Richard could see the excitement in Tom's eyes at the prospect and smiled to himself. Oh yes, everything was going to be alright now. "Why don't ye go and tell

Jenni that we're going to the mine while I finish my coffee?" suggested Richard tilting his head to the side. "Don't forget to tell her that Mary and the girls will be along in a bit to collect her and the bearns."

Tom immediately rose to his feet. He was eager to see the Mine and equally anxious not to be there when Jenni saw where they would be living.

"Aye good idea," said Tom. He went out of the dining room and along the hallway to their room. He only hoped his mother could convince Jenni that the dugout would be alright in the short term.

Chapter 23

Richard and Tom stepped out of the hotel into the cool foggy morning air. Richard slung his bag over his shoulder as he pointed out the hill that was directly opposite them. "That's where the Mine is, right under that hill. Come, tis only a short walk from here."

Tom stood looking for a moment before they started walking up the street towards the Mine. After a short distance, they crossed the road and Richard picked out a well-worn path which led straight up the side of the hill. They climbed the hill in silence, but by the time they reached the top Tom could clearly hear the familiar sound of a loud Cornish beam engine. They paused at the top and Tom got his first look.

The mine was situated in a hollow that he thought covered an area of about ten or twelve acres. He could see numerous shafts and buildings as well as huge piles of copper ore spread about. It was a hive of activity with men in red shirts going this way and that, and boys busy in the sorting sheds. He grinned at his father.

"Well, tis bigger than I thought. They don't call it the Monster Mine for nothing."

"Aye, they do not. Wait until ye get underground though," replied Richard leaning closer to be heard above the ruckus. "It isna as deep as some mines back home, but it covers a larger area methinks. To get to the pitches I want ye to look at we'll go down Kingston's Shaft." He started heading down towards the carpenter's shop with Tom at his heels. "That's the crusher on your left there, and we'll just go to the right past the main ore floor," said Richard pointing out the huge waterwheel and crushing house.

They were just approaching Kingston number two shaft when someone called out to Richard. "Hey, Bryar!"

Richard turned and immediately recognised the tall bearded man who was approaching him. "Ah tis Captain Roach," he said turning back to Tom. "He's the head captain."

Richard smiled warmly as the Captain came nearer. "Captain Roach nice to see ye. This here's my son, Tom just arrived from Cornwall."

Captain Roach extended are large hand in Tom's direction and smiled warmly at him. "We can always do with experienced men. Welcome to Burra Burra."

Tom shook the Captain's hand. "Thank ye."

"Now I've good news for ye," he said turning his attention back to Richard. "The Company's constructing twenty tenements for the newly arrived folk, and I thought you'd want to be the first to know. Shall I put your name down for one then?"

"Oh aye, I canna tell ye how happy my wife will be when I tell her," replied Richard shaking the Captain's hand. "Can ye spare one for my son and his family as well?"

Captain Roach looked Tom up and down before a smile spread across his face. "Awright, I think I can spare one for ye as well. Good day to ye both," he said before continuing on in the direction of the dressing sheds.

Richard stared after him for a moment. "Your mawther is going to be beside herself with happiness when we tell her the good news. She hasn't been happy since we came." He glanced at Tom. "Come on, this way."

They skirted around the front of the dressing sheds until they came to the open shaft where they could descend into the mine. Richard dropped his bag on the ground and pulled out two hats and candles. He handed one to Tom along with a lump of soft clay. "The first level's down two hundred feet or so," he said moulding the clay around the candle and attaching it to his hat. "I'll see ye at the bottom then."

"Aye," replied Tom fixing the candle to his hat and lighting it. He waited until his father had descended through the hole and started down the ladder before following him. It took a few moments for his eyes to adjust to the gloom below ground, but in no time he was nimbly navigating his way down the ladder. It had only been a few months since he was last down a mine, and so the feeling that he was suffocating took him by surprise. He instinctively sucked in several large lungfuls of air as he traversed the final few feet.

"Are ye awright?" enquired his father looking at him oddly.

"Aye," replied Tom as he regained his composure and began breathing normally again. "Tis just the lack of air. It took me by surprise is all."

Richard knew well enough what he meant. The mine had several large air shafts, but there wasn't as much oxygen as they were used to. "Aye. It took me by surprise when I first came down as well. Don't worry, ye willna notice in a day or two."

It took Tom a few moments for his eyes to adjust fully to the dim candlelight. They were standing at the bottom of the shaft in a large open gallery. Copper ore glinted from the floor and walls in bright colours of red, green and blue and Tom grinned stupidly. "'Tis just as Philip Downing said. Is it not?"

Richard grinned back at him. "Aye, more or less. As I said it costs more to haul the ore out of here than it does back home." He looked around the gallery. "But, there is certainly more of it. Come on, we'll need to go down another couple of levels to look at the first pitch."

Tom followed his father as they made their way to the shaft that would take them down to the lower levels. There weren't any miners working this section of the mine. As Richard explained it had only recently been excavated by the tut workers and contained new pitches which were yet to be worked. They followed a narrow tunnel that had been reinforced with timbers until they came to the first pitch. The tunnel was quite wet and water continually dripped from the ceiling. Tom wondered how far down the water table was here in South Australia, but didn't mention it.

Richard had been busy counting his steps and checking a hand-drawn map of this section of the mine. "Here it is, pitch forty-three," he said coming to halt. "According to my calculations, we should be able to clear eighteen pounds each if we can get it at the right price. What do ye think?"

Tom stepped closer for a better look. The pitch had been surveyed the same as it was done back in Cornwall, and so it was quite familiar to him. It was about sixty feet deep and thirty feet wide. There was a wide vein of copper ore running through the middle of it, which would be easy to mine. What Tom couldn't be sure of was if the vein would continue or diminish in size as they mined it.

"Ye would know better than me Da how far back the lode is likely to go. But, if the vein goes back a ways then it should be a good pitch," replied Tom walking the length of the pitch and back again. "I don't think we should bid less than eight shillings."

Richard looked at him thoughtfully and nodded in agreement. "I've only worked the one pitch since we arrived. The lode has been fairly constant, but that doesna mean that this one will be," he said. "I agree with ye though, we shouldna take it on for less than eight shillings."

"Have ye got any idea what the Captain is likely to take for it?"

"Aye. He doesna want to pay more than seven shillings and sixpence. But, if no one else bids he'll have to pay more methinks," replied Richard. "Don't worry, there are several more good pitches to look at. Come on."

They spent the rest of the day inspecting potential pitches. They were generally in agreement on which ones they would bid on come survey day next week. Richard was confident they would be successful in getting a good pitch at the right price. Tom wasn't so sure, but as he had no experience with the Burra Burra Mine he would agree with whatever his father decided.

"My preference is for pitch twenty-nine if we can get it for ten shillings," said Tom as they made their way back down the hill towards town. "But, I'll be happy with whatever ye decide."

Richard slapped him on the back. "Good. I'm glad ye trust me," he said smiling happily at his son. "Come on, I'll buy ye a pint to celebrate your safe arrival."

Tom grinned back at his father. An ale or two before they went home was a very good idea. He was in no hurry to deal with Jenni and the dugout.

Chapter 24

Jenni and the girls were just finishing their breakfast when Mary, Alice and Maryann arrived. Jenni sighed contentedly. It was just so good to be surrounded by them once more. She felt safer than she had done since arriving in Adelaide, and was happy to allow the women to take charge of her and the bearns.

"Where's the baby?" enquired Mary looking around the dining room and then at Jenni with a quizzical brow. "What have ye done with her?"

Jenni smiled. "Don't worry. Louisa kindly offered to watch her while I had my breakfast. She willna be far away." She took a sip of tea and popped the last morsel of toast into her mouth.

"Sit next to me Grammer," insisted Beth patting the chair beside her encouragingly.

Mary smiled warmly at Beth and kissed the top of her head. "Awright, but just for a moment. We've come to take ye all home," said Mary as she sat down beside her.

Susan was about to protest at her Grammer sitting beside Beth, when Alice scooped her into her arms and sat down as well. She popped a slightly appeased Susan on her lap. "Aye, twill be so good to have ye all settled in with us. We've missed ye all so much, haven't we Maryann?"

Maryann pulled an extra chair over and plopped herself down as well. "Aye, we've missed ye all like mad."

Jenni was bursting with happiness at seeing them all so enthusiastic about them moving in with them. It was going to be a bit cramped for everyone, but she was sure they'd have their own house in a few weeks.

"So, tell me about the house. I imagine we're all going to be squeezed in a bit," said Jenni leaning forward in her chair. "Not that I mind. I'm ever so grateful that we don't have to stay in lodgings."

Mary gave her a bit of a queer look. "Did Tom not tell ye about it then?"

"No. He just told me that ye would be along to collect us after breakfast. He was ever so excited about seeing the Mine with his faather," said Jenni taking the last mouthful of tea. "Ye know how he is. He's been so anxious about it."

Mary nodded, but Jenni couldn't help but notice an odd glance pass between her mother-in-law and her daughters. She looked from one to the other but couldn't work out what was going on.

"Is there something amiss?"

Mary smiled nervously. "No there's naught wrong. It's just that...well...Tom was supposed to tell ye about the house." She paused while she tried to contain her rising ire. She was sure Richard would've told Tom about the dugout, but maybe he hadn't made it clear to Tom that he should warn Jenni. She would give Richard what for when she saw him. "I sent Richard to speak with him about it, and I canna believe they didna tell ye."

Jenni was getting worried now. The letter Richard and Mary left for them in Adelaide had hinted that they weren't in a proper house. And now Mary was suggesting that Tom should have told her about it. Where were they living? Not in a tent surely. Her worried expression must have been obvious, because Alice was now looking somewhat alarmed. On the other hand, Maryann had found something very interesting on her lap. She was avoiding even looking in Jenni's direction.

"Ye have to tell her Ma," interjected Alice. "I'm sure Jenni will understand."

"Aye," put in Jenni looking Mary square in the eye. "Whatever it is ye better tell me. Ye are making me very nervous."

Mary licked her lips and nodded. "Aye. Well, where to begin." She twisted her fingers together nervously in her lap. She wouldn't blame Jenni one bit if she just wanted to go straight back home to Cornwall. If that was the case, then she wouldn't be far behind her.

"Just tell her Ma," insisted Alice raising her voice.

Jenni looked from one to other and tried to quell her rising apprehension. "Please, Mary. Are ye living in a tent? Is that it?"

Mary shook her head. "Not a tent," she almost whispered. "Tis an underground dugout down by the creek. Tis dug into the creek bank."

Jenni looked at her incredulously, before glancing at Alice and Maryann. The look on their faces confirmed it.

Alice slumped in her seat and gave Jenni a look of dismay. "Tis just awful Jenni, but we've made the best of it. We're warm enough, but it does get a bit damp at times."

"A dugout?" said Jenni finally finding her voice. 'Like a hole in the ground?"

"Are we going to live in the mine?" asked an excited Beth.

"No we are not," replied Jenni sternly.

"Look it isna as bad as it sounds, really," said Mary with a sigh. "We have a tin roof and the walls are whitewashed. We don't have a proper floor, but we could put down some rugs for the bearn. Twill be a little cramped. We thought we'd put Beth in with the girls, but Susan and Esther will have to be in with you and Tom." She paused while Jenni digested the reality of their situation. "It willna be for long. Richard is doing his best to get us a house to rent, but there just aren't any right now."

Jenni's mind was racing with what she imagined this was going to be like. She had just come across the sea on a voyage lasting several months, followed by weeks getting here on the horrid mail coach. She didn't see how she had any other choice but to try and make the best of this. There was no way she could bring herself to turn around and go back home. The mere thought of Mr Opie's coach was enough to stop her in her tracks. She took a deep breath and clenched her teeth together determinedly.

"Alice would ye go and find Louisa and fetch Esther please," she said calmly. Alice nodded and passed Susan over to Maryann before departing on her errand. "I think the best thing to do is for me to see this hole in the ground. Surely it canna be as bad as I imagine."

Mary gave her a resigned smile. "None of us are happy about it Jenni. The girls and I just hate it, and if ye decide not to stay then we'll go with ye."

Jenni leaned across the table and squeezed Mary's arm affectionately. "I hope it willna come to that."

.~.

If Tom was disheartened by his first glimpse of the dugout he could only imagine how Jenni was feeling about it. After what had been an exhilarating day seeing the Burra Burra Mine for the first time, the scene that he now witnessed tore his heart. Jenni was sitting with Esther in her arms, her red-rimmed eyes and dishevelled appearance bearing testament to her impression of their home.

He looked around at the dirt floor and whitewashed walls. It really was just a hole in the ground. He had no idea how his father and mother had managed living here since their arrival.

Jenni looked up at him with accusing eyes. "Why did ye not tell me?"

He felt helpless and shrugged. "I swear I only found out about this myself this morning." Having not seen the dugout until right this minute, he couldn't have told her about it anyway. His father had made it sound alright. A little bit damp, but otherwise habitable. Now that he'd seen it for himself though, he didn't like the idea of his wife and children living here for any length of time.

"Oh tis not that bad," said Richard coming to stand beside his son. "Anyway, we have good news. We'll be getting a house to rent as soon as they're built. The Company's building twenty new tenements and we're to get one each."

Mary swung around from the stove where she was stirring a large pot of stew. "Ye are not serious? Truly. We are to get a house?"

"Oh, Da that is such good news," said Alice looking up from the game of marbles she was playing with Beth and Susan.

Maryann and Lizzie stopped setting the table and gawked at their father. Lizzie had a huge grin on her face, and Maryann ran and hugged him. "Oh, Da ye have no idea how much I have hated living here."

"I like it here," chimed in young Richard.

"Well, twill likely be a few months, but we should be settled in a proper house afore Christmas." Richard crossed the room and swept Mary into his arms. "Twill be awright now, I promise ye."

Mary wiped tears of happiness from her face. "Well, twill be awright as long as Jenni will stay." She turned to her daughter-in-law. "Ye will stay won't ye?"

Tom looked at his wife in alarm. He hadn't seriously thought she might not want to stay. He hoped Jenni remembered the promise they'd made.

Jenni rocked Esther back and forth and kissed the top of her head before looking at her mother-in-law. "I don't want to stay here."

Tom hurried across the room to her side. He knelt beside her and looked her in the eye. "Ye canna mean it, Jenni. After all, we've been through to get here. And we don't have the money to repay our fares, let alone have enough to buy passage back home. We canna leave."

She gave him a withering stare. "Aye. But neither can I or our bearns stay here." She looked around the room with distaste and grimaced. "Ye canna expect us to."

He had to admit their situation was unexpected. He wasn't thrilled about spending the winter in a damp underground dugout either, but what choice did they have. Tom looked around at the rest of his family who were all looking at Jenni apprehensively.

"Please Jenni," he said. "Surely ye can see that we have no choice. And tis only for a short while. We'll be in a proper house afore ye know it."

She turned her anguished eyes on him. "Tom, I canna put Esther down on this floor." Large tears leaked from the corner of her eyes and ran down her face. She quickly wiped them away with the back of her hand. "I'm sorry, but I canna stay."

Mary came to her side as well and put a comforting arm around her shoulders. "No one blames ye for not wanting to stay. I expected as much, and was so afeard that ye would want to go back home. But Jenni, Tom is right. ye canna go back."

Jenni nodded. "Maybe not. And I'm not saying I want to go back to Cornwall. God knows I couldna get on that coach again." She shuddered. "But surely ye can all see that the bearns canna stay here."

"We can do something about the floor if that's the problem," said Richard looking at his wife for support. "We can put down more rugs for the bearn."

"Aye of course we can," said Mary. "Twill be awright Jenni."

Jenni sighed. She really thought Mary and Richard would understand how she felt, but they didn't. "I'm afeard for my bearns if we stay here. I thought ye would understand. After all, ye lost five of your own. I canna bear the thought of it."

It finally dawned on Tom. Jenni wasn't concerned about living in a dugout as such. She was worried for the children. Well, he had to agree it was a bit damp, but the rest of his family had been living here since April and they were fine. He was sure she was overreacting. How could he convince her that the girls would be fine? He wasn't sure he could.

Mary stepped back from Jenni, the pain and hurt clear in her eyes. "Jenni we would never put our grandbabies in danger. We love them like they were our own bearns. I canna believe ye would think that of us." She returned to the stove and began vigorously stirring the pot of stew. "If ye want to go we willna stop ye."

Jenni rose to her feet and stared at Mary's ramrod back. "Earlier today ye said ye would stand by me and my bearns. Ye promised to go with me if I didna stay."

It was now Richard's turn to look alarmed. "Is this true Mary? Tell me ye didna make such a promise?"

Mary turned to face her husband. "Aye I did, but I see now that I shouldn't have done so."

Jenni didn't wait to hear anymore. She turned on her heel and headed for the small back room that she would be sharing with Tom and her two youngest daughters. She tucked Esther into her cot before collapsing on the bed. She couldn't stop the torrent of tears that followed. She had never wished for her mother more than she did right now, but at the same time was so glad that she wasn't here. She had no idea what she was going to do. She let out one final sob and wiped the tears from her face. After taking several large breaths of air she managed to regain control of herself.

"Are ye awright Jenni?' said Tom as he quietly approached her and sat on the bed.

She turned her tear-stained face to him. "No I am not awright, and I don't know what to do. I am just so afeared for our bearns."

He gathered her into his arms. "I know, but twill be awright. I wouldna put ye or our bearns in danger, ye know that," he crooned softly. "Ma and Da have lived here for several months now, and everyone is just fine. No one is ailing."

She sighed. "I know ye wouldna put us in danger. But look around Tom," she said gesturing. "Tis a hole in the ground, and Esther is only six months old. I fear something will happen to her. She is such a small sweet thing."

"Awright...I willna argue with ye, Jenni. Tis not an ideal place to live, but tis only temporary," he said letting her go and looking into her eyes. "If ye want to leave then we will. I can probably get work at the mines in Kapunda. Twill mean a return journey on Mr Opie's coach though."

Jenni was torn. She knew how much Tom had been looking forward to working at the Burra Burra Mine with his father. It was the whole reason they'd immigrated in the first place. She groaned.

"I don't know what to do."

"Come and have supper then, and sleep on it. Maybe in the morning, it willna seem so bad."

All eyes immediately turned on Jenni as they entered the kitchen. She could see the question clearly written on all their faces. Was she going to stay? Maryann was the first one to approach her.

"Please stay Jenni," she said. "We're family, and we'll all help ye with the bearns. Ye will see, they'll be awright."

Lizzie was putting down plates of piping hot stew and potatoes. "Aye Jenni, ye must stay. Come and sit here," she said gesturing to an empty chair.

Jenni smiled weakly at them both. "Thank ye. Tom has convinced me to stay for the night. We will decide what to do in the morning." She sat down at the table next to Susan and tried to ignore the hostility she could feel emanating from other members of the family.

Richard finally took his place at the head of the table. Once everyone else had taken their seats he bowed his head and said grace. This included more than a few words of thanks for the safe arrival of Tom and his family. Jenni felt sure this was directed squarely at her, but she was determined not to succumb to more tears.

Supper was awkward, to say the least. Jenni concentrated on helping Susan eat hers so she didn't have to engage in conversation. Not that there was much of that going on. Tom and his father were discussing their strategy for winning a good pitch. Mary barely looked at her, and certainly didn't offer any consoling words. She had to concede that she didn't have anything more to say to her mother-in-law either.

Chapter 25

The next day dawned grey and gloomy, which reflected Jenni's mood perfectly. A fitful night's sleep hadn't helped and her head was pounding. She finished feeding Esther before heading out to the kitchen to prepare breakfast for the girls.

She was surprised to see they were already sitting at the table hoeing into bowls of porridge slathered in honey. When Tom saw her he rushed to her side and gave her a warm hug.

"Good morning," he said. "Come and sit, I'll get ye some porridge." He felt her hesitate. "Don't worry I didna make it. Maryann made it afore she went to work."

She smiled at him. "Thank ye," she replied as she sat down next to Beth. "Where is everyone?"

"Well, Da's gone to the mine of course. Alice and Maryann are working at the hotel today, and Lizzie and young Richard have gone to school," he replied putting down a bowl of porridge in front of her. "Ma's running some errands."

Jenni had the distinct feeling that everyone had vacated the house early on purpose. Well, that was probably good. It would give her a chance to talk to Tom.

Tom sat back down to finish his breakfast. "Have ye decided Jenni?" He didn't mean to beat about the bush. "I meant what I said last night. If ye wants to leave we'll go to Kapunda."

She pressed her lips together as she tried to find the right words. "I don't want to do that to ye, Tom, ye know I don't," she said putting down her spoon. "But, it doesna seem any better to me this morning than it did last night."

He sighed. "Well, tis decided then. We'll have to stay until I can make arrangements. We'll send our baggage ahead, and I'll see if we can get on Mr Opie's coach when he comes back next week."

Jenni nodded. The thought of getting back on Mr Opie's coach was almost enough to make her change her mind. Almost, but not quite. She was feeling unexpectedly guilty, but not enough to overcome the fear she felt for her children. She hated what this would mean for Tom and wished they could stay.

"Awright," she said. "Perhaps we could come back in a few months once the new houses are ready."

"We've barely enough money to get to Kapunda," said Tom looking his wife squarely in the face. "Ye have to be sure about this Jenni. We willna be able to come back."

She didn't have to think about her decision for long as she gazed around the room, and then at her two daughters. "I'm sure."

Tom appeared to accept her decision. She was sure he was disappointed, but he was a man of his word. She knew he would do all he could to get them to Kapunda.

He reached out and squeezed her hand reassuringly. "Twill be awright Jenni. I can work just as well in Kapunda as I can here. My faather will be most disappointed, but he will get over it," he said smiling at her. "If we could just stay until survey day. I know Da would really appreciate that."

She nodded. She was well aware that Richard would want Tom with him come survey day. The two of them had talked of almost nothing else. "Aye. We'll go after survey day then."

"Thank ye, Jenni."

Two-year-old Susan had been too preoccupied with spooning porridge into her mouth to pay much attention to her parent's conversation. However, Jenni now noticed that Beth was staring at them both open-mouthed. "What is it, sweetheart?"

"Aren't we staying here with Grammer?"

"We'll stay for a few days," said Tom to his eldest daughter. "Then we'll go back to Kapunda so I can get some work in the mine there."

She looked at him perplexed. "But I don't want to go."

"Well I'm very sorry about that Beth, but you'll get to spend a few days with Grammer afore we go," he said smiling at her. "Twill be awright you'll see."

Jenni put a comforting arm around her and hugged her close. "I'm sorry we canna stay as well, but ye needna worry about leaving just yet."

.~.

Tom opened the door to the Burra Hotel and went inside. He was pleased to see that Mrs Barker was at her desk in the foyer and smiled. "Good morning to ye Mrs Barker."

She looked up from the booking register and smiled warmly at him. "Mr Bryar? You're Alice's brother aren't you," she said obviously pleased with herself for recognising him. "You must be so glad to be reunited with your family. I know Alice was just so excited that you'd all arrived safely."

Tom was at a loss for words for a moment. "Oh...aye," he finally managed to say.

"Well if you're looking for Alice, I think she's in the dining room," she said going back to her register.

"Ah no, actually I was wanting to speak with you, Mrs Barker. I believe ye take care of the bookings for Mr Opie's coach service."

"Yes that's right," she said looking up at him. "Did you want to make a booking Mr Bryar?"

"Aye. For my wife and myself and our three bearns. We'll be returning to Kapunda, a fortnight from now if that's possible."

If she was surprised by his request she didn't show it. She pulled a small book out from under the counter and opened it.

"Well now let me see," she said flipping through the pages. "Well, it looks like you're in luck, Mr Bryar. Mr Opie should be departing here on Tuesday the seventh of July. Shall I put you down?"

Tom breathed a sigh of relief. That would be perfect. "Aye please do. Thank ye, Mrs Barker."

He finalised the booking and paid their fares. All he had to do now was arrange for their baggage to be taken to Kapunda. All the bullock teams would be fully loaded with copper ore; none of them would likely have room for his trunk and sea chests. He would have to come up with another solution.

"I wonder Mrs Barker if ye would know of anyone that could take our baggage to Kapunda?"

"You'd best speak with some of the bullock teamsters up at the mine. They'd most likely help you out."

"Oh, I think they'd be fully loaded with ore, Mrs Barker."

She smiled at him. "You're new to these parts. No. Come the first of July the roads will be closed for the winter season. Meaning, they won't be hauling any copper or coal until the spring."

"Thank ye, Mrs Barker," he said surprised. Maybe he'd be able to hire Mr Hastings again. "I'll take your advice and ask up at the mine."

"Glad to be of assistance," she said going back to her register.

Tom left the hotel and headed back to the dugout. He was anxious to assure Jenni that he'd booked their return journey to Kapunda for two weeks from Tuesday. He was feeling apprehensive about telling his father they were be leaving. He also hoped that his mother would mend the rift between herself and Jenni before then.

.~.

After supper that evening, when all the bearns were tucked into bed Tom finally approached his father.

He stood beside Jenni's chair with his hand draped protectively on her shoulder. "Jenni and I have come to a decision," he said nervously. "It hasn't been easy, but we've decided to go to Kapunda. We leave in two weeks." He felt Jenni tense beneath his fingers and tightened his grip.

Richard sighed and ran his fingers through his hair. "I don't blame ye, but can ye not just wait a bit?"

Mary tensed and pressed her lips together, but didn't enter into the conversation. Tom knew his mother was unhappy about their decision and would find it difficult to accept. He just hoped she'd understand that it was for their bearns.

"Jenni has agreed to wait until after survey day. I promise ye I'll be there for that Da," he said sitting down beside Jenni. "We just hope ye will both understand that we canna stay."

Richard put his arm around Mary's shoulders. "Aye, of course, we understand Tom. But we have all come so far from home, to not stay together now seems like such a pity. If ye could just wait a bit," said Richard leaning forward and looking into his son's eyes. "We'll be in a proper house in no time at all. Don't rush off to Kapunda, the bearns will be just fine. I promise ye. Please will ye not reconsider?"

Tom looked at Jenni to see if she was likely to change her mind. Her soft grey eyes looked back at him with steely resolve. He sighed. "I'm sorry Da, I've already booked us onto Mr Opie's coach.

We'll send for our other belongings once we're settled."

"We're truly sorry that we canna stay," said Jenni taking hold of Tom's hand. "And I hope ye will not hold it against us."

"Of course not," Richard assured her. "Tis just that I feel ye are rushing into this decision after only one day here. Tis really not as bad as it first appears. If ye could just wait a bit afore deciding. Give it a couple of weeks, then if ye still decide to go we'll give ye our blessings."

Tom nodded. "Well, twill be a couple of weeks afore we leave at any rate. If it doesna seem so bad then we may change our minds by then," he said. "I don't want ye to get your hopes up though. I don't think we'll change our minds."

"Awright, I canna ask ye for more than that," said Richard.

Chapter 26

Kooringa 30th June 1857

Over the next week, life settled down to some semblance of normality. Richard hoped Mary would put her hurt aside and make peace with Jenni before they left for Kapunda. Even more, he prayed Tom and Jenni would change their minds and stay. In the meantime, though, he had more important matters to deal with. It was survey day.

He took a sip of his coffee. "The bidding will start at noon, but we need to be there afore that," he said to Tom who was seated at the table opposite him. "I hear Hutchen's intends to bid for pitch sixteen, so I think we should try for twenty-nine and not bother with the earlier ones. What do ye think?"

"Aye. It may limit our choices somewhat, but we can always try for forty-three if we miss out. Twill be a good pitch if ye can get it at the right price," said Tom. "Have ye got any idea what the Captain wants for twenty-nine?"

"No, he's been tight-lipped," said Richard taking another mouthful of coffee. "Understandably, he doesna want to show his hand too soon methinks."

Tom nodded. He'd had dealings with Captain's back in Cornwall who would withhold the price until survey day. Captain Roach was obviously experienced at setting the value of new pitches. He just hoped they'd be able to secure one for a fair price.

Richard finished his coffee and stood up from the table. "Twill be awright as long as Ellis and Kinsey are happy with the bid," he said turning back to face Tom. "They've put their trust in me to get a good contract. I only hope I don't disappoint them."

"Ye can only do your best Da, and they know ye will," said Tom draining the last of his coffee as well. "I'm only sorry I willna be here to work it with ye."

"Aye, well there's naught to do about that."

They kissed their wives and the bearns farewell and headed off to the mine. The bidding would be taking place outside the Mine Office, and so they made their way directly there. The winter sun wasn't providing any warmth and a few clouds were scudding across the sky. A stiff breeze was blowing from the south and the air was freezing. Richard pulled the collar of his coat up around his ears as they joined the throng of miner's outside the office.

They didn't have wait long for Captain Roach and his offsider, John Paull to emerge and mount a small elevated platform. A table had been placed on the platform along with a dish of small pebbles.

"Good afternoon to ye gentlemen," said Captain Roach greeting the assembled miners. "Now afore we begin, ye should know that the takes will be expiring on the 25th of August. They are the same as usual, in that the bid amount will be paid on dressed ore to the value of twenty shillings." He paused for a moment. "Ye will be responsible for extracting the ore and delivering it to the nearest shaft where it will be hoisted to the surface. The cost of hauling, weighing and dressing will be deducted from the contract price. Any other costs incurred by ye for candles, gunpowder and such will also be deducted on settlement day. Are there any questions?"

Apart from a few murmurings and shuffling of feet all was quiet. "Awright then. Subsist pay of two pounds per man will be paid upfront by Mr Paull for each successful bid," said Captain Roach. "Now for the first pitch. Number seven - four shillings." He picked up a small pebble from the dish and waited for the first bid.

All was quiet for a moment, then one of the miners near the front of the crowd called out his name. "Brenton."

Captain Roach threw the pebble in the air. By the time it landed no one else had entered the bidding and so John Brenton won the take.

"Excellent Mr Brenton," he said smiling. "Mr Paull will take down the details of the take." He took another pebble from the dish and called the next pitch. "Number twelve, nine shillings and sixpence."

The auction continued at a brisk pace. Richard and Tom bided their time until the Captain called for bidding on the pitch they were most interested in. "Number twenty-nine...ten shillings."

Richard immediately stepped forward. "Bryar," he called.

No sooner had he made his bid than Henry Pinch also stepped forward. "Pinch. Nine shillings and eleven pence."

Captain Roach tossed the pebble in the air. Richard waited a split second before calling his second bid. "Nine shillings and ten pence."

A moment later Pinch called his second bid "Nine shillings and sixpence."

For one heart beating moment, Richard thought he had it. The pebble hit the ground and Captain Roach called "Pinch by a whisker."

"Don't worry Da," said Tom patting his father's reassuringly. "If ye can get forty-three twill be awright."

Richard nodded. Aye, it would be alright, but if he missed out on forty-three his choices would be severely limited. He'd have to take one of the pitches that had been handed in without a bid. He groaned. Henry Ellis and Will Kinsey would not likely thank him for that.

The auction continued. If there was one saving grace it was that there was less and less competition for the remaining pitches. Richard took heart and determined to win forty-three.

"Number forty-three," called Roach. "Seven shillings and ninepence."

Richard hesitated for no more than one moment. It was threepence less than he would have liked, but any work was better than none. "Bryar," he called.

Captain Roach looked at the remaining miners to see if anyone else was going to bid. All was quiet. He tossed the pebble in the air and Richard held his breath.

It landed and Richard let out the breath he'd been holding. Well, he had a pitch, and he thought Ellis and Kinsey would be happy enough with the price.

Tom thumped him on the back. "Well done Da. I reckon ye have a decent pitch there."

"Aye," said Richard grinning back at him. "I hope so. We've come such a long way for it." He strode up to the table where John Paull was taking down the contract details.

"How many in your pare?" he enquired with his quill poised.

"There'll be three of us," replied Richard.

"That'll be six pounds subsist pay," he said taking the money from a small tin and sliding it across the table towards Richard. "Do ye understand the terms of the contract Mr Bryar?"

"Aye."

"Well, please sign or make ye mark here," he said turning the contract book around to face Richard.

Richard signed his name and picked up the six pounds. He breathed a sigh of relief. He felt like he'd finally arrived. The only sour note was that Tom wouldn't be working the pitch with him. He returned to his son's side.

"Come on, Will and Henry will be expecting us at the pub. I'll buy ye a pint."

Chapter 27

Burra Burra Mine, 3rd July 1857

Tom agreed to work the pitch with his father until he left for Kapunda the following Tuesday. They'd spent the last couple of days drilling and packing holes with gunpowder ready for blasting. Will Kinsey and Henry Ellis had agreed to do the blasting last night, and Richard and Tom would get the first load of ore to the plat this morning. From there the ore would be hoisted to the surface and the first samples taken.

Richard and Tom climbed the hill to the mine in silence. It was a still and frosty morning, and Richard rubbed his hands together to keep them warm. He was anxious to get the first load of ore to the surface this morning and prayed the sampling would go well.

"I hope the blasting went well last night," said Tom as they approached Kingston's Shaft. "We should have a good load of ore ready for hauling if it did."

Richard pulled his hat out of his bag and fixed a candle to the front of it. "Aye. I'm a little anxious about the sampling, but ye are right. We should be able to get a good lot hoisted to the surface today."

Tom was putting his hat on when he noticed what looked like smoke coming out of Stock's Shaft. "Da, is that smoke?" he said pointing.

"Aye, it looks like it," said Richard looking up in alarm. Smoke was billowing out of the shaft. There was only one thing that could cause that. Fire.

"Go and rouse the Captain. I'll head down and see what's amiss."

"Be careful Da," Tom said over his shoulder as he headed for Captain Roach's cottage.

Richard lit his candle and clambered down the ladder into the mine. It took a few minutes to climb down to the main gallery. He looked around. There was no sign of smoke and everything seemed fine. He headed north until he came to a tunnel that led down to the twenty-five-fathom level. For smoke to be coming out of Stock's Shaft, he figured the fire had to be down on the lower level.

As he neared the shaft he heard the roar of the fire. He hurried down the narrow passage which was filled with smoke. It stung his eyes and he coughed as he took in a lungful of it. In the gloom and smoke, he couldn't see down the passage at all and hoped there weren't any men down there. He called out but doubted anyone would hear him.

He hesitated for a moment, before pulling his shirt up around his nose and mouth. He continued on until he saw the blaze. The support beams were on fire and had created a tunnel of flames. He coughed several times as the smoke threatened to overcome him.

Two men were lying face down on the ground and he rushed towards them. The first man he came to appeared to be unconscious. He rolled him onto his back and grabbed him by the shoulders. He dragged him as far away from the flames as he could. He coughed again and wiped his eyes which were now streaming down his face. He resisted the urge to suck in a large lungful of air. The smoke was getting thicker. He took in several shallow breaths before deciding what to do.

The other man was lying further along the tunnel. He'd have to pass under one of the burning beams to reach him. There was still no sign of Tom or the

Captain. No one else had come to
investigate either. He looked at the burning
beams and thought if he bent down low
enough he could pass underneath them
without getting burnt.

He tried to steady his breathing and
calm his nerves. Without another thought,
he ducked down and ran down the tunnel.
The air was hot and the heat of the fire
threatened to force him back. He was
determined to continue on. He was almost
crawling by the time he reached the other
miner. He grabbed him by the shoulders
and started to drag him to safety. The man
groaned.

"I've got ye," said Richard coughing
again. "Hang on."

It was difficult dragging the man
while staying low to avoid the beams. His
shoulders were screaming for him to stop,
and his legs were starting to feel like they
had no strength left. He could barely see in
the thick smoke and through his tear-filled
eyes. He stopped for a moment to catch his
breath. He was feeling dizzy and slightly
nauseous. He sat down beside the man and
tried to clear his head.

He was panting and having
difficulty catching his breath. The dizzy
feeling was making him feel confused and

disoriented. Try as he might he couldn't clear his thoughts. He tried to stand up, but his legs refused to hold him. He thought he heard someone calling him. It was the last thing he remembered as he slipped into unconsciousness and slumped over the man he'd been trying to drag to safety.

.~.

Mary's legs felt like jelly as she ran up to the door of Doctor Mauran's cottage. It served as his home, consulting rooms as well as the hospital for the mine. She pushed opened the door and hurried inside. Her heart had leapt in her breast when she'd received word that Richard had been overcome by smoke in the mine.

He was alive but unconscious. Fear surged through her now that she was here.

"Ma." Tom grabbed her and hugged her close as soon as she stepped through the door. "Are ye awright?"

"Aye," she said pulling out of his grasp. "Where's your faather? Is he awake yet?"

"He's through here," he said indicating to a closed-door at the end of the short hall. "He's not awake yet, just as well."

She looked at him in alarm. "What do ye mean?"

"Doctor Mauran says the burn on his arm is bad. He's with him now."

She pushed Tom aside and opened the door at the end of the hall. Doctor Mauran turned and looked at her quizzically as she entered. He was a tall gangly man with greying hair and a pair of wire spectacles on the end of his nose. "I thought you might've been my wife."

"Doctor Mauran, I'm Mary Bryar. My husband was injured at the mine today," she said peering around him to see where Richard was. He was lying on his back on one of the narrow beds. Another miner was lying unconscious in the other hospital bed.

Without waiting for the doctor to respond, she hurried to Richard's side. His face looked blotchy and there was soot all around his nostrils and mouth. He appeared to be having difficulty breathing. Every breath sounded slow and hoarse. Her insides squirmed as fear threatened to overcome her.

"Will he be awright?"

Doctor Mauran ignored her for a moment and continued bandaging Richard's arm. "It's too early to say, madam," he said turning his round brown eyes on her. "I've treated his burns, but as for how much smoke he's inhaled...well..we'll have wait until he's awake."

"Aye. Will that be soon?" she said looking at Richard's closed eyes.

"It's difficult to say," he replied as he finished fastening the bandage. "It may be a while. You can stay if you wish."

"Thank ye, Doctor, I'll stay until he wakes." She pulled a chair up beside the bed and sat down. She took a couple of deep breaths and blinked back the tears that were threatening. Taking hold of Richard's hand she prayed.

Doctor Mauran checked his other patient whose breathing also sounded laboured to Mary's ears. "I'll be back to check on your husband again soon. Call me if he wakes," said Doctor Mauran. Without another word, he left the room.

A few minutes later Tom came in. "Is he awright Ma? What did the Doctor say?"

Mary shook her head. "I don't think the Doctor knows. We'll have to wait until he wakes up, and he doesna know when that will be." Putting her head in her hands she succumbed to the tears that she'd been holding back.

Tom rushed to her side and put his arms around her. "Hush Ma. Twill be awright," he said. "He's a strong man, he'll come through this. I know it."

Mary gave one last sob and wiped the tears away with the back of her hand. "Aye. What if he doesna?"

Tom swallowed the lump in his own throat. "He will."

Chapter 28

Mary awoke with a start. She was disoriented for a moment until she remembered where she was. She'd fallen asleep with her head on her arms leaning on Richard's hospital bed. She quickly checked her husband. He was awake and blinking at her with red-rimmed eyes.

"Richard! Oh thank God," she cried. "Tom your faather's awake, call the Doctor."

Tom hurried across the room to his father's bedside. "Da. Oh, ye are awright."

"Call Doctor Mauran," repeated Mary.

Tom nodded and hurried out of the room.

Richard moaned as he tried to sit up. "Don't move Richard. Ye have been badly hurt and unconscious for hours. Stay still until the Doctor comes," said Mary pushing him gently back down.

"Is he awright?" asked the woman sitting by the bed of the other injured miner.

Mary hadn't noticed the woman and she took her by surprise. "Oh aye I hope so," she replied before she got to her feet and went over to introduce herself. "I'm Mary Bryar. I don't think we've met afore."

"Pleased to meet ye," the woman replied. "I'm Sarah Temby. This 'ere is my husband William."

"How is he?"

"Well thanks to your husband he's alive," she replied. "But he hasn't woken up as yet."

"Well, hopefully, it willna be too long now. My husband Richard has only just this minute opened his eyes." She looked back over at Richard who had closed his eyes again. She didn't think he'd slipped back into unconsciousness; his eyes were probably painful. They looked swollen and were scarlet around the edges and very bloodshot.

Doctor Mauran came bustling into the room with Tom right on his heels. He went immediately to Richard's bedside. "Can you hear me Mr Bryar?" he enquired peering at his patient.

"Aye," he croaked opening his eyes once more. He coughed several times before managing to catch his breath. He groaned.

"Hm. I'd like to listen to your chest Mr Bryar," said Doctor Mauran as he helped Richard into a sitting position. "How would you describe your breathing? Does it feel constrained?" he asked as he put his stethoscope to Richard's chest and listened intently.

"Aye. It feels tight and it hurts when I cough," replied Richard hoarsely. "My head hurts something fierce."

"Yes. I'll get you some laudanum for that," said Doctor Mauran peering closely into his eyes. "You've breathed in quite a bit of smoke and it'll be some days before you're breathing easier." He pushed a pillow behind Richard so that he could recline back against it. "You'll find it easier to breathe if you're partially sitting."

The Doctor went to the door and called to his wife. "Bring the charcoal and tincture of milk thistle."

He stopped and checked on Mr Temby, who was still lying unconscious in the other bed. He gently lifted his eyelids and inspected his dilated pupils. "He should be waking soon," he said to Mrs Temby. "Just be patient a little longer."

She smiled weakly at him.

Mrs Mauran came into the room carrying a tray of medicines. It contained a jar of black charcoal and a small vial of dark liquid. She placed it on the side table and then proceeded to mix several spoonfuls of charcoal with a small cup of water which she handed to Richard.

"Here," she said smiling at him. "This will help you to breathe easier."

Richard took the small cup and looked at the black liquid before gulping it down. He grimaced and then looked slightly surprised.

Mrs Mauran smiled at him. "It doesn't taste as bad as it looks does it?" she said taking the cup from him. "I can't say the same for the tincture."

She returned a moment later and gave him a spoonful of the tincture, and a dose of laudanum.

Doctor Mauran came back over to Richard's bed. "The best thing for you now is rest. It'll take a few weeks for you get your strength back."

Richard nodded and closed his eyes. "Thank ye, Doctor."

"We'll go and let ye get some rest then," said Mary kissing him gently on the forehead. "We'll come back and see ye later."

"Good idea Mrs Bryar," said Doctor Mauran. "If there is any change in his recovery I'll send you word."

Once again Mary felt alarm spread through her. Surely he was going to be alright. "Is that likely Doctor? I thought he'd be awright now."

"No doubt he'll continue to recover Mrs Bryar," replied the Doctor calmly. "But, sometimes there can be complications. If there is I'll let you know."

"Come on Ma," said Tom putting his arm around his mother's shoulders. "Let Da get some rest. The Doctor will look after him."

"Aye," she nodded and allowed Tom to lead her towards the door. "Our prayers will be with ye and your husband as well Mrs Temby," she said stopping by the other bed. "I hope he wakes soon."

"Thank ye."

Tom and Mary left the doctor's cottage and started on their way home. Mary was exhausted. She'd been on edge all day and was still uncertain as to how Richard was going to recover from this. Obviously, he wasn't going to be able to work for several weeks. She wondered if Henry Ellis and William Kinsey would be able to work the pitch alone. Even if they could, she wouldn't see any money from it. It all threatened to overwhelm her. She took a couple of deep breaths, while she decided on her best course of action.

"Tom, I know ye and Jenni are to go to Kapunda on Tuesday," she said glancing sideways at him. "But I wonder if ye would consider staying until your faather is well enough to go back to work? Twould only be a couple of weeks."

Tom put his arm affectionately around his mother. "Aye, I've been thinking about that. Don't worry, we'll stay until Da's back on his feet."

"Oh thank ye, Tom," she said smiling up at him. "I canna tell ye what a relief that is. I'm worried enough about your Da without worrying about the pitch as well."

"I know ye have enough on your plate," he said. "Leave Ellis, Kinsey and the pitch to me. Ye just worry about Da."

.~.

They arrived home and were immediately inundated with questions from Jenni, Lizzie and young Richard. Mary sat down and heaved a massive sigh. Of course, the whole family was worried sick about Richard, but Tom could see his mother was exhausted.

"Go and have a lie-down Ma," said Tom "Jenni can take care of supper, and I'll keep an eye on young Richard. Go, get some rest afore we go back to the hospital."

"No I'm awright," she said getting to her feet. "Tis best if I keep busy."

"How's Da?" demanded Lizzie. "Is he awright? Can we go and see him?"

Young Richard was nodding in agreement with his sister's questions. "Aye, I want to go and see Da too."

"Da's awake, and the Doctor says he needs to rest," explained Tom patiently. "That means ye canna go and see him just yet. Don't worry, he's awright. He's just very tired."

Jenni poured boiling water into the teapot. "Sit down Mary, at least let me get ye a cup of tea. Ye don't need to worry, I've already started supper."

Mary smiled at her. "Awright, thank ye, Jenni. I'll have a cup of tea." She went and put her arms around her youngest children. "Don't worry, your faather is going to be just fine. If he's up to it, I'll take ye to see him tomorrow. Awright?"

"Awright Ma," said Lizzie hugging her mother. "I was just so scared when Jenni told us that Da was hurt."

"I know I was scared too. We must thank God that he's awright," said Mary. "We must also pray that Mr Temby will be awright. I think he's hurt worse than your Da."

"Whose Mr Temby?" asked young Richard.

"He's the miner that Da pulled from the fire," replied Tom. "Da's just lucky the Captain and I arrived when we did."

After his father had gone down the shaft, Tom headed across the ore floor to the Mine Office. He rapped on the door and peered in the windows. No one was there. His heart sank.

His mind was racing as he tried to decide what to do. He was just stepping off the veranda when he noticed a line of cottages behind the Office. They either had to belong to the Captain's or at the very least someone of authority.

He ran towards them and hurried up the path to the first one. He had no idea which one belonged to Captain Roach. Without hesitating, he rapped on the door. It was opened a moment later by a short sandy-haired man.

"Can I help ye?"

"Aye. I need to find Captain Roach," he replied barely able to contain his urgency.

"If he's not already at the Office, his is the next cottage along," said the sandy-haired man. He leaned out of the doorway and pointed to the stone cottage next door. "I'm Captain Mitchell, can I help ye with something?"

"I really need to speak to Captain Roach. There's a fire," said Tom pointing towards Stock's Shaft. "My faather's gone down to investigate."

Captain Mitchell immediately looked in the direction of the shaft. "Good Lord," he exclaimed. "Aye, ye go and fetch Captain Roach. Tell him I'll gather a few of the men and meet him down there." He snatched his coat off the peg by the door and sprinted down the front path. "Hurry up man," he called back over his shoulder at Tom who was still standing by the door.

Tom ran down the path to the next cottage and pounded on the door. He bounced up and down impatiently on the balls of his feet while he waited. No one came. He knocked again, and called, "Captain Roach."

The door was finally opened by a young boy who yawned tiredly at him. "Yeah?"

Tom was momentarily taken aback. "Is Captain Roach at home?"

"Aye. Who shall I say's calling?"

"Well, that doesna matter. Tell him there's a fire in the mine. I need to speak to him."

"Awright," replied the boy.

He shut the door and left Tom standing on the doorstep. He wondered if he was fetching the Captain or not. Tom's nerves were beginning to feel like someone had stretched them into an archer's bow. He stood there waiting for what seemed like an eternity, his stomach getting more and more tied up in knots. His anxiety was just about reaching the limit when the door opened again.

"What's the problem?" said Captain Roach looking Tom up and down. "Ah, I remember ye. Your Richard Bryar's son aren't ye?"

"Aye." Without bothering with any further polite conversation, he blurted out, "there's a fire in the mine. My faather's gone down to see what's amiss."

"A fire?" replied Captain Roach as he scanned the horizon. He had no trouble seeing the smoke and steam that was billowing out of Stock's Shaft.

"I ran into Captain Mitchell on my way over here. He says to tell ye that he'll fetch a few men and meet ye down there."

"Right," said Captain Roach slamming the door shut behind him. "Come on then."

The Captain hurried down the path with Tom almost running to keep up with him. They were just passing Schneider's Engine-house when someone called out.

"Captain Roach," called a short balding man. "A moment if ye please."

"Not now Penno," replied the Captain without slowing his gait. "Whatever it is will have to wait."

Tom thought the man's ruddy complexion went even ruddier. Quite undaunted he hurried along beside them. "It canna wait Captain, not if the engine's to keep going."

The Captain came to a halt. "Alright, Penno. What seems to be the problem then?" he said with a sigh.

Penno stopped and caught his breath. "Aye, well I was expectin' a delivery of coal yesterday and it didna come. I reckon I can keep the engine going at slow speed for a couple of hours at most."

Captain Roach groaned. The last thing he needed was supply problems with the coal. A few years back they'd had to almost close the mine due to a lack of fuel for the winter.

"Well I canna help ye with that right now, I've got a bigger problem to deal with," replied the Captain. "Go and see if Captain Goldsworthy can sort out the deliveries. Tell him I sent ye."

"Aye thank ye, Captain, I'll do that," said Penno. He scratched his beard thoughtfully, "should we keep on pumping out the forty fathoms level?"

"Aye," replied the Captain. "And when ye see Captain Goldsworthy tell him there's a fire in Stock's Shaft." He didn't wait for any further response from Penno, but slapped Tom on the back and started walking towards Kingston's Shaft. "Come on, we've no time to lose."

They hurried across to the shaft and Captain Roach descended the ladder first. Tom waited until he was a good way down before he started down as well. He was worried about his father. It seemed to have taken him ages to find Captain Roach and for them to get down the mine. He knew how dangerous fires in a mine could be. Miners frequently left candles too close to the support timbers and they caught alight. Most of the time they were extinguished before they became a problem. However, Tom knew a large fire could suck the oxygen out of the mine in no time. He hoped his father hadn't gotten too close to it.

He finally reached the bottom of the ladder and the main gallery. His eyes were only just adjusting to the gloomy light when the Captain lit his candle and put his hat on. "Here, let me light yours as well"

Tom leaned forward so that Captain Roach could reach his candle. Tom straightened as it flickered to life.

"Alright let's go then," said the Captain extinguishing the match. He started heading north in the direction of Stock's Shaft with Tom at his heels.

They hurried down to the twenty-five-fathom level, and before Tom saw the shaft he could hear the roar of the fire. His stomach clenched with fear at the sound of it. The tunnel was full of suffocating smoke and he pulled his shirt up over his face.

Up ahead of Captain Roach he could see the flames. The timbers were well alight and lying not far from them were two men.

Another man was propped up against the wall of the tunnel well clear of the flames.

It was only as they ran towards the two men that Tom realised one of them was his father. "Da!"

Fear gripped him as he took in the scene - his father was on fire. His hat had come off and his candle had caught his shirt on fire. Captain Roach reached the two men before Tom and was already stamping out the flames when he reached his father's side.

"Da! Are ye awright?" He knelt beside his unconscious father and shook him.

"We need to get them out of here," said Captain Roach coughing as he breathed in a lungful of smoke.

They dragged Richard and the other miner as far from the flames as they could. Tom was sweating profusely and coughing uncontrollably by the time they'd dragged the two men clear. His eyes were streaming down his face and he was starting to feel dizzy. Captain Roach didn't look a whole lot better.

Tom sat down next to his father and tried to stop his coughing and catch his breath. He and the Captain both leaned against the walls of the tunnel panting.

Tom could hear voices and turned his head just in time to see Captain Mitchell emerge out of the smoke. He was accompanied by eight other men, some of whom were carrying picks.

"Are ye awright Captain?" he enquired kneeling beside them.

"Aye, we're fine. We need to get these men out of here though," said Captain Roach wheezing. "Send a couple of the men to get planks so we can stretcher them out."

"Aye," said Captain Mitchell. "We'll have to block off this pitch and let the fire burn itself out."

Captain Mitchell quickly took control of the situation and sent several men off to fetch makeshift stretchers. In the meantime, he and the other men moved the unconscious men further along the tunnel. Tom got to his feet and followed the men who were carrying his father.

As soon as they were clear of most of the smoke they put him down and Tom sat down beside him. He put his ear to his chest. He could hear his heart beating. Tom let out a massive sigh of relief. If they could get him and the other men out of the mine soon he was sure they'd be alright.

Captain Roach and one of the men arrived carrying the other miner who'd been found next to his father. They put him down beside Richard.

"Are ye awright Tom?' asked the Captain peering at him.

"Oh aye," he replied looking up at him. He imagined he must look just as soot-stained as the Captain did. "I just hope we can get these men out of here soon."

"Aye, we will. Just as soon as the men come back with the planks." He leant down and put his hand on the unconscious man's chest. He was breathing, but only just. "I hope they hurry. Poor George here looks like he's in a bad way."

Tom glanced at the man. He had to agree he looked deathly pale beneath his red and blotchy face. "Do ye know him?"

"Oh aye," replied the Captain. "Tis George Johnson, he works the Grenfell pitch. He's got a wife and a young bearn." He indicated to the other man lying beside them. "And that's Will Temby."

"Well, I think they're probably lucky my faather came along when he did." He was worried though. They needed to get them out of the mine and into the fresh air soon.

"Aye," said the Captain nodding in agreement. "It looks like he dragged them away from the fire."

Several men appeared out of the gloom carrying makeshift stretchers. Thank God thought Tom. He helped them lay his father on one of the planks and then secured him with some ropes. They did the same with Johnson and Temby. The Captain then went back down the passage to get help carrying the injured men.

Captain Mitchell and several of the men returned with him. Tom took one end of the stretcher that his father was on and they started towards the nearest plat. Tom wasn't familiar enough with the mine to know which shaft was the nearest. However, they were heading away from the fire, and it was so good to be out of the smoked filled tunnel.

When they arrived at the shaft the winch had already been lowered. They secured George Johnson to the whim first, and Captain Roach gave the signal for them to start raising him to the surface. Tom couldn't imagine how frightening that would be. Just as well he was unconscious.

It took another hour before all three men had been safely raised to the surface and taken to the Mine Hospital. Tom was exhausted. He slumped in a chair and prayed for his father and the other two men.

Chapter 29

Mary popped a cup of tea on the small table at Richard's elbow. He was sitting in the parlour by the window, a woollen rug tucked around his knees. He was looking better than he had done in weeks, and Mary hoped he'd be back on his feet soon.

He smiled at her. "Thank ye, Mary."

She sat down in the other chair by the window and picked up her mending. "You're welcome."

Esther was on the floor nearby kicking her feet in the air and cooing to herself. Mary smiled at her. She couldn't remember the last time she'd felt so content. After months in the awful dugout, they were finally in a proper house. They were crammed in, and nobody had any privacy, but Mary didn't care. Tom and Jenni would be in their own house soon enough, and then there would be plenty of room.

There was just one thing to mar her happiness. The guilt she felt every time she thought of Mrs Johnson. Her husband

George hadn't been as fortunate as Richard and William Temby. After hours down in the smoke-filled mine, he was the first one they winched to the surface. They'd rushed him to the hospital, but within the hour he'd succumbed to the smoke and died.

When his young widow was told of his demise she was beside herself with grief. They'd only been married a couple of years and had a small bearn, barely a year old. Mary's heart went out to her, but at the time was too worried about Richard to offer the poor young woman much sympathy.

Three weeks later Captain Roach had come to the hospital to discuss things with Mary and Richard. "Ye know ye can't go back to that dugout," he'd said. "Your lungs have been badly damaged by the smoke, and the damp will see ye off for sure."

"I thank ye for your concern Captain, but where else do ye expect me to go?" Richard had replied grumpily.

"Well, I have a proposition to put to ye both," he'd said ignoring Richard's bad mood. "Mrs Johnson's decided to go to Adelaide to be with her sister. That means I've got a vacant house. She doesn't want to be bothered with the furniture either, so I think if ye make her a fair offer she'd accept it."

"A house? Ye mean for us?" Mary had interjected excitedly.

"Aye, that's exactly what I mean."

"Oh, Captain! I canna thank ye enough for thinking of us first," Mary had said. She was very sorry Mrs Johnson had lost her husband, but there was naught she could do to change that. She was well aware that if Richard returned to the dugout in his current state of health he might not see the winter out. He'd developed a terrible wheeze which Doctor Mauran had assured her was temporary. Still, she couldn't help but worry.

"Well, I think your need is greatest. You'll take it then?"

Mary hadn't given Richard a chance to reply. "Aye, we'll take it."

"You'll take it will ye?" Richard had said scowling at them both. "And what about Tom and Jenni? Have ye forgotten that they'll be leaving for Kapunda afore long? We canna move out of the dugout and leave them there."

Mary moaned impatiently. "No, I haven't forgotten about Tom and Jenni. They can move into the house with us." She'd turned her attention fully on Captain

Roach. "They can move with us can they not Captain? Their new house will be ready afore long won't it?"

"Well, it would certainly be a bit cramped for ye all, but of course they can move in with ye." Captain Roach had run his fingers through his beard thoughtfully. "The new houses are only a couple of months off being finished."

"There ye go," Mary had said with a satisfied look on her face. "Tis settled. There is no way ye are going back to that dugout, Richard."

Richard had groaned with frustration. "They willna be needing a new house, Mary. They'll be leaving for Kapunda as soon as I'm back on my feet."

"Maybe. Maybe no," she'd replied. "The only reason they wants to leave is because of the bearns in the damp. If we all move into the house that the Captain has kindly offered us, well – they might not leave Richard."

Richard had looked at her doubtfully, but her excitement couldn't be dampened. Mary was sure if they could just get them out of the dugout then Jenni would agree to stay. She was confident that as a mother she understood her daughter-in-law's worry for the bearn's. All she had to do was present her with a solution and all would be well.

A week later they'd moved out of the dugout and into the cottage in Church Street. It was a four-roomed weatherboard cottage on the end of a row of four. The front garden was somewhat overgrown and untidy, but it had a neat and tidy back yard with a separate wash house and clothesline. The kitchen was more like a lean too tacked onto the back. It had a combustion stove and was large enough for a table and dresser.

The rest of the house consisted of a front parlour and three bedrooms. Young Richard was sharing Richard and Mary's bedroom, and Beth was in with the girls. Susan and Esther were sharing with Jenni and Tom. It was all very cramped but as Mary looked around the parlour, she couldn't have been happier.

The best news of all was that Tom and Jenni had decided to stay in Kooringa. Their new house would be ready for them to move into in another couple of months. As far as Mary was concerned everything had worked out just perfectly.

Richard was getting stronger every day, and Tom was happy enough working the pitch with Ellis and Kinsley. At least they would have some money from the current take. Mary just hoped Richard would be back to full strength by next Survey Day.

Laughter from the front yard reached her and she looked out the window at Jenni and girls. They had been weeding the garden but appeared to now be engaged in a game of ring around the rosy. She smiled to herself. Yes, everything had worked out just perfectly.

The End

Author Notes

Thank you so much for reading my book. I'm an Australian indie author. As such, I maintain complete control of my work and self publish. That also means I have to market and promote my work, which I'm not very good at. I find it hard to self promote.

So, I'm taking this opportunity to not only thank you for taking the time to read my book, but if you liked it, would you mind leaving a rating or review on Amazon. It's the best way to show any author that you appreciate their hard work. It also helps other potential readers to decide if they should invest their time and money.

You already know that I write historical fiction, and you may have also realised that my stories are based on the lives of my ancestors. I've been passionate about family history for many years, and I've discovered so many amazing ancestors who led such interesting lives. So, I blend fact with fiction and bring their stories to life, and I'm so excited to be sharing them with you.

If you enjoyed this book, please consider reading one of my other titles.

Thank you

For the love of Family

The story of the Bryar family continues in Book 2 of the Copper Road series.

Family life is full of trials and tribulations, and the Bryar family have their fair share. There are weddings and the arrival of new family members, as well as sadness and loss.

After several years working the monster mine in Burra, Richard and his son Thomas decide there are better opportunities in the new mines at Wallaroo. Tom never seems to be satisfied and yearns to make his own way in the world.

He makes the fateful decision to try his luck in the coal mines of Newcastle. Following his arrest for unpaid debts, his family are ashamed of him. It all comes to a head one night with disastrous consequences. Can they mend the rift, or will Tom and Jenni look for new horizons?

Jacob's Mob

How did one fateful decision land Aaron Price in New South Wales as an assigned convict?

He and his mate James were best described as petty criminals until they decided to try their hand at breaking and entering. What started as a grab for easy money, ended with them being sentenced to transportation to the colonies for life. Aaron may be lamenting his fate and the fact that he won't be seeing his sweetheart again, but is he content to serve his sentence?

Aaron knows only too well that bushranging is a hanging offence, and yet he once again allows himself to be persuaded. On the run and eager for revenge, he and his new mates wage terror on their previous master and the other settlers of the Hunter Valley.

However, Aaron isn't content to just wreak havoc - he's got an escape plan. If only he could find a way to get himself on board a ship bound for America. The British have no jurisdiction there, and he would be free.

Based on the true story of Aaron Price, who arrived in New South Wales in 1825 on board the convict transport Guildford.

Margaret

From Bredgar House to Van Diemen's Land.....

Margaret Chambers never imagined she'd be forced to flee her family home and country to escape a hideous old man and an arranged marriage. Pretending to be a general servant she boards a ship bound for Hobart Town. It's 1837, and in order to get free passage out to Van Diemen's Land, she's agreed to work for Mrs Hector. There's just one problem, she's never done a day's menial work in her life and her lie is soon discovered.

Taken into the household of the Reverend Davies and his wife Maria, she not only finds kindness but friendship, and is employed as Maria's companion. She couldn't have hoped for a better situation, but when convict and scoundrel William Hartley crosses her path will it all come tumbling down? Seduced by the young and charming William she finds herself unable to remain with the Reverend and his wife. Maria doesn't want her to go but Margaret can see the conflict between Maria and her husband. Not wanting to be the cause of any rift between them she leaves.

William still has five years of his seven-year sentence to serve and he's not free to marry her. However, he stands by her side by stealing food for her and his unborn child until he gets caught. Sent away to work on the chain gang Margaret's left to fend for herself. Somehow she finds a way to survive until William's free to join her and when he gets a Ticket of Leave and permission to marry her, the future's looking hopeful.

C J Bessell

Printed in Great Britain
by Amazon